THE NIGHT THEY CAME HOME

A WESTERN HORROR STORY BASED ON
ACTUAL EVENTS

JOHN A. RUSSO

WOLFPACK
PUBLISHING
— EST 2013 —

The Night They Came Home
Paperback Edition
© Copyright 2022 John A. Russo

Wolfpack Publishing
5130 S. Fort Apache Rd. 215-380
Las Vegas, NV 89148

wolfpackpublishing.com

Paperback ISBN 978-1-63977-933-8
eBook ISBN 978-1-63977-932-1
LCCN 2022935063

"The Rufus Buck gang were childish and vicious, innocent in their naiveté and brutal in their outlook." — Leonce Gaiter

THE NIGHT THEY CAME HOME

1

On March 17, 1895 a hanging took place at Fort Smith, Arkansas, in a courtyard crowded with thousands of rudely dressed farmers, ranchers and townspeople. There were few women and almost no children in the gaping, gawking crowd. Clusters of rudely dressed roughnecks passed bottles around, drunk and getting drunker, because to them a gruesome hanging was the best kind of entertainment. Many of them had ridden here on horses or in wagons or had walked on rutted trails through miles of hot, dusty countryside to arrive in high spirits for this great and boisterous event.

The notorious Fort Smith gallows was a huge, efficient death machine. Twelve wooden steps led up to the twenty-foot-wide wooden platform. A thick overhead beam spanned it from end to end, and the trapdoor beneath it could drop twelve men at a time, if need be, but today there was only one featured guest. His birth name was Crawford Goldsby, but he was known far and wide as Cherokee Bill. He was only eighteen years old but was known to have killed at least eight men. He started his string at age twelve by shooting his own brother-in-law for ordering him to do something he didn't want to do: feed the hogs. Deemed too young for prosecution, he was sent to the Indian School in Carlisle, Pennsylvania, but ran away at age fifteen and fled back to the Wild West to start a vicious crime spree that terrorized people for three years. After a slew of hold-ups and shoot-outs, he was captured and sentenced to death for the murder of a federal marshal during an attempted train robbery.

As Bill mounted the platform, shackled and prodded by two armed jailers, the vengeful gawkers crowded as close as they could get to the foot of the gallows and heckled and jeered at the top of their lungs, making it clear to him, as if he didn't already know it, that in their eyes he richly deserved what was about to happen to him.

When the official Fort Smith hangman, George Maledon, dropped his thick noose over Cherokee Bill's head, a great raucous cheer went up. Maledon was a macabre celebrity, not only in the local community but all across the United States, thanks to a chain of articles in *Frank Leslie's Illustrated Newspaper* that had dubbed him the *Prince of Hangmen*. He had hanged fifty-six men in the past twenty years. In his early sixties now, and suffering from lumbago, he always ignored the pain and went about his work with a deep and zealous pride. He was a small man, only five six and one hundred and fifty pounds, with a leathery face and a flowing white beard, and he always wore a black suit, a black tie and a black stovepipe hat. In case anyone doubted that he meant business, he had a black ammo belt buckled tightly around his waist and two pearl-handled revolvers holstered on his hips, with the handles facing outward, not in, easy to pull them out with his arms crossed.

Maledon's pal Heck Thomas stood by him with a pistol and a shotgun, his cold gray eyes scanning the mob for any signs of trouble, such as a foolhardy attempt to rescue Cherokee Bill from execution. Heck was wearing a wide-brimmed hat, a brown flannel shirt, denim trousers and tall scuffed boots. His shiny long-barreled .45 Colt revolver was holstered not on his hip, but at the front of his stomach. When Maledon had once asked him why he wore his pistol that way, he said it prevented any evil-minded scoundrel from coming up on him from behind and too easily snatching it away from him.

On the opposite side of the trapdoor from Heck Thomas and George Maledon, Judge Isaac Parker stood by with his Bible. He was in his early sixties and had pronounced all of the fatal sentences that George Maledon had carried out, plus dozens more that were carried out by some of his substitute hangmen while George was away, chasing outlaws. The judge had a thick mane of white hair, a bushy white mustache and a flamboyantly luxuriant white goatee that was a striking contrast to his somber black suit and black string tie. The yellow journalists who called Maledon the Prince of Hangmen called Parker *The Hanging Judge*. Up on the platform, he appeared to be unarmed, but sometimes he had a derringer up his sleeve, in spite of his stern belief that nobody would dare harm him while he was doing the Lord's work.

When he opened his Bible, the crowd quieted to a low hum of ramped-up enthusiasm and drunken murmurs. But Judge Parker didn't read his accustomed passage from Ecclesiastes, *a time to reap and a time to sow, a time to live and a time to die...* Instead he paraphrased a death sentence once recited by Judge Roy Bean that he thought was particularly apt today:

"Crawford Goldsby, otherwise known as Cherokee Bill, you have slaughtered eight men that we know of, and one of them was a prison guard right here at Fort Smith that you shot while trying to escape. Therefore I say to you that in a few short weeks it will be spring. The snows of winter will melt away, and the air will be sweet and balmy. But you won't be here to see it. The spring flowers will put forth their tender shoots, but you won't be here to smell them. Butterflies will sport in the sunshine and bees will pollinate the bright golden flowers. But you will not be here...no, you will not be here. Because today you are getting what you so richly deserve, you murderous scoundrel, which is to hang by your neck until you are dead."

Cheers and applause burst from the gawking crowd.

Judge Parker said, "Crawford Goldsby, do you have any last words?"

"You wicked son-of-a-bitch, I came here to die, not to make a speech!" the condemned man said. "And today is as good a day to die as any other!"

With that, George Maledon pulled a black bag over Cherokee Bill's head. Then, without further ado, he pulled the lever, and his victim plummeted to his death through the trap door that barely made a sound on its well-oiled hinges. Bill kicked just once and then dangled limp and still under the gallows platform, where the people could gape at him all they wanted. At the same time, murmurs, gasps and cheers went up from the crowd. The drunks passed their bottles around and swore and guffawed to show that a hanging didn't bother them one bit. And for a time after that, the mob continued to mill around, staring at the dangling corpse while it was being taken down and laid face up onto a stretcher.

Aided by armed deputies pushing people aside to make way for them, Judge Parker and Heck Thomas shoved their way through the diminishing crowd while George Maledon retrieved his rope, then descended the twelve steps down from the gallows, where he was meekly tapped on his shoulder by a mousey-looking man in a frayed and rumpled brown suit. "Excuse me, Mr. Maledon," the man said. "I'm Seth Crosby...if you remember. I'm the reporter who spoke with you yesterday. Can we do your interview now...I mean, if you have time, sir."

Maledon stopped and thought for a moment, then said, "Let's do it in my cabin."

The cabin was made of unpainted rough-hewn planks, and had a single room with a bunk bed, a roll-top desk and a bentwood chair with no cushion.

"Excuse the sparse accommodations," George Maledon said. "I'm not here much. Most of my time is spent chasing down bad guys for the bounties on 'em."

Seth Crosby suppressed a shudder as he stared at the collection of leg irons, straps and ropes that were part of the hangman's trade. He watched Maledon as he took off his stovepipe hat and hung it on the same peg that supported a dangling noose.

"You wanna use my chair, Seth?" Maledon turned and said. "I'll sit on my bunk."

"Uh...I'll use the bunk, sir," Crosby said uncertainly. And as he sat, he took a pencil and notepad out of his vest pocket.

Maledon wryly took note of the fact that the reporter looked as though he couldn't wait to get out of there.

The meek little man was soft and pudgy, maybe about forty, in no shape to get in a fist fight. But his mousey brown hair showed no gray yet.

"Was today your first hanging?" Maledon probed.

"Yes...sir."

"Queasy, are ya?"

Seth Crosby tried to say something, but failed.

Maledon pulled one of his thickly coiled ropes down from its peg and showed the reporter its tightly wound noose. "I've used this one here in eleven hangings," he explained. "It's made of the finest hemp fiber, hand crafted in St. Louis and specially treated to keep it from slippin'. People think you want a slippery knot, but you don't, because a slippery one will just strangle, it won't break the neck. You wanna feel it?"

Crosby looked as if he was going to faint. His hands shook when he tried to write something in his notebook.

"You see," said Maledon, "a big knot is necessary to have a humane hanging. If it doesn't break the man's neck when he drops, then, again, he strangles, and it goes on and on and takes a long, long time. That ain't a pretty sight, Seth. Makes his tongue stick way out and turn purple, and his eyes bulge damn near out of their sockets. And he kicks and twists a lot. I don't want that. No, no."

Crosby gulped, took several deep, panicked breaths, then tried to change the subject. "Er...like I told you, Mr. Maledon...I'm writing for *Frank Lesley's Illustrated Newspaper*, and I'm sure my article will be very widely read and could be turned into a bestselling series of dime novels."

"How much money could somethin' like that fetch me?"

"Well, could be three or four thousand dollars in

royalties, just for you, Mr. Maledon. But I don't want to get on Judge Parker's mean side."

"Why?" Maledon shot back facetiously. "He's not gonna sentence you to death by hanging if you cheat me outta my royalties."

Crosby didn't smile, just nervously licked his lips, then said, "I know he hates being called the Hanging Judge and his court being called the Court of Damnation. And I expect you're probably touchy about it, too."

"Nope. I'm not. I never hanged a man who didn't deserve it. They drop right through, just like Cherokee Bill did, and don't even twitch. Not like that sloppy job that dumb-ass hangman in New Mexico did on Black Jack Ketchum. The rope tore his head right off. I'd be ashamed of myself if I did a thing like that right in front of the honest law-abiding citizens."

Crosby gulped, looking like he wanted to turn green. Then he said, "Well, sir, not to change the subject on you, but I'm thinking that my article won't be about the... er... executions...you've carried out under the law. I'm thinking about concentrating on the killers you've hunted down. People don't know enough about that, and it'd elevate you in their eyes."

Just then there was a loud knock on the cabin's door, and a jailer burst in, all in a dither.

"Judge Parker wants you and Heck Thomas in his office right this minute, George!" the jailer blurted. "John Garrett's been gunned down!"

"Gotta go," Maledon said to Seth Crosby as he got up from his bentwood chair.

2

Ten-year-old Tommy Palmer tingled with excitement when he woke up this morning, because he was getting to go with his dad on a twenty-mile wagon ride all the way to Fort Smith. For a boy living on an isolated ranch, this was like a journey to someplace exotic. He was glad they didn't go yesterday because then it would've been already over with instead of yet to be anticipated. He had badly wanted to go yesterday, but his dad didn't want him to be there when Cherokee Bill was being hanged. Even though he didn't see the hanging, he hoped he would get to hear some gossip about it. He had a wistful curiosity about what it would have been like, and he knew that if he *had* gotten to see the hanging, he would have been envied by all the kids in his one-room schoolhouse, come fall when they would all be telling each other what they had done during the summer. But at least he could say that he hadn't chickened out, he had simply been forbidden to go.

Yesterday, after hearing him say for the hundredth time how he wished his trip to the fort would hurry up and get here, his grandpa had taken him out to do "big people's work" on the family ranch. At age sixty-three, Grandpa Jake Warner was tough and wiry and brooked no nonsense from anybody, and Tommy loved, admired, and badly wanted to please him. Together they went out on horseback to spot mavericks or "sleepers." A maverick was a calf that had weaned itself without being branded or earmarked, and a sleeper was a calf which had been earmarked but not branded. The earmark for the Warner ranch was two V's cut into the tops of the calves' ears. If a cow thief could spot a weaning calf before it had been earmarked and branded, he could notch the ears, hoping its rightful owner would assume that it had also been branded, then after the calf was weaned the thief could steal it by burning in his own brand and cutting the ears into a different shape.

Spotting sleepers and mavericks required sharp eyes and plenty of patience, and Tommy wanted to show his grandpa that he was up to it. All morning long, he found nothing worth bragging about. But after a noon lunch of beef jerky and tepid water, he spotted a maverick, and he and Grandpa Jake built a small fire and got the calf branded and earmarked.

Then they rode off in different directions, and Tommy came upon a full-grown cow in grave danger. She must have been trying to drink from a stream, had waded in too far, and had gotten herself hopelessly mired in sticky mud. She was in so deep that her nose was barely above water. Tommy yelled for his grandpa, because he knew that if the cow wasn't rescued in time she would either drown or have to be shot.

Grandpa Jake came galloping, and when he saw what was happening, he yelled, "You're gonna have to help me, Tommy! I can't do it alone!"

But Tommy was scared and didn't know exactly what was expected of him. He stared wide-eyed as his grandpa dismounted and hurriedly took off his gun belt, chaps, boots, spurs and hat. Then he waded into the stream and swam breaststroke out to the marooned cow, carrying a coil of rope in his left hand. And when he got to the stranded cow, he looped one end of the rope over the animal's horns, then tossed Tommy the other end of the rope.

"Tie it around your saddle horn!" Grandpa called out. "Then start backing your pony off to make the rope tight enough to hold the cow's head above water!"

Tommy did what he was told, even though he was a little shaky over this brand-new experience. Then Grandpa surface dived and went under. He re-surfaced with gobs of mud in his hands. Then he gasped for breath and dived under again, while the cow started mooing loudly and mournfully. Grandpa kept surface diving and going under, and after he managed to claw enough of the mud loose from the cow's hooves, she floated helplessly at the end of the rope, like a ship without a rudder. She sagged over onto her side and rolled her eyes, a sign that she had given up. Grandpa got hold of the cow's tail and twisted it, trying to get her to float upright while he was holding her nose up so she could breathe. But he was having a hard time in the sticky mud and waist-high water.

Desperately, Tommy dug his spurs in and got his pony to start backing up some more. To his great relief, as if the pony finally realized what was expected of it, it dug in its hooves and started towing the cow to shore. As soon as the cow touched dry land, she scrambled to her feet, lowered her horns, shaking off the rope, and charged off, bellowing loudly, as if she wanted to gore somebody.

Grandpa waded his way out of the stream, and he and Tommy laughed their butts off while the old man stood there, stark naked. Tommy knew that now he would have a funny story to tell the kids at school, come fall.

That evening, when they got back from hunting for mavericks and sleepers, he and his grandpa told the stranded cow story to his parents and his grandma, exaggerating it only a little, and they all got a big laugh out of it. That night, as he tossed and turned upstairs in his bunk bed, anxious for morning to get here so his trip could begin, Tommy strained to hear what Dad and Grandpa might be saying about Cherokee Bill and the murders he had committed, while they were smoking hand-rolled cigarettes downstairs at the kitchen table, but they kept their voices so hushed that he couldn't make out the words.

This morning over eggs, bacon and cornbread, Tommy and his grandpa milked the cow story for a few more laughs. Thoughts of Cherokee Bill's hanging the day before were melting away but Tommy's excitement about the trip to Fort Smith was in full force. He could barely wait to get done gathering eggs in the chicken coop while his father was hitching a horse to the buckboard. After he rushed his basket of eggs into the house, he ran out with his little duffle bag, which he had packed a few days ago just to make the trip seem more real and more imminent, and tossed it into the bed of the wagon while his dad was tightening the harness.

"I'm all ready to go, Dad!" he called out exuberantly.

"Hold your pants on!" his dad said.

Tommy's dad, Chuck Palmer, was a stubble-bearded and ruggedly handsome man in his early forties. When he was a boy his hair was as blond as Tommy's, but later it had darkened to a sandy brown, and was now flecked with strands of gray. In Tommy's eyes, his dad was every bit as tough and commanding as Grandpa Jake, and Tommy hoped that as he reached adulthood he'd turn out that same way.

Grandpa Jake said, "Well, c'mere and give us a big hug!"

He bent low enough for Tommy to get his arms around him, while Grandma Clara waited to get her own turn. Tommy could feel her soft round ball of a stomach under her flowery apron. Her iron-gray hair was rolled up in a bun, and Tommy had never seen her wear it any other way. But when she washed it, she took it down and let it dry while it hung all the way past her waist.

Tommy's mother, Clara, and his sister, Jolene, came out of the house carrying a big wicker basket by its handles. Clara was wearing a well-worn calico dress, and Jolene, age fourteen, was in jeans and a homemade denim blouse. Her sandy hair was in pigtails, which her mother usually braided, against her objections. She thought she looked more grownup with her hair down.

Clara and Jolene put the hamper into the wagon under the driver's seat, and Clara came over to Chuck and hugged and kissed him, quickly because people were around. Backing off, she told him, "We packed enough food for two days. It'll even last for three, if you have to stretch it. I mean, in case you get held up. There's some jerky you can chew on, in a pinch."

Tommy hugged his mother, because she held her

arms out, expecting it. She kissed his cheek, making it wet.

Dad told her, "You worry too much, Clara. Fort Smith is only twenty miles away. We'll be there by nightfall, stay overnight at my parents' house, buy all our winter supplies in the morning, then head back here. Tomorrow night leave a porch lantern burning for us, we'll be here, guaranteed."

Grandpa said, "Soon as we hear that buckboard comin' we'll put coffee on. Right, Lucy?"

Grandma Lucy said, "I'm gonna bake a chocolate cake tomorrow, too. I think I've got enough flour to do it. It'll be waitin' for you. I'm glad you'll be bringin' me some more flour before I run out."

Jolene got all puckered up and pleading and said, "Why can't I go with you, Daddy? I haven't been to town since last March."

Chuck said, "Next time you can come with me, and Tommy can stay home. This time you'll help your mom and grandma with the canning, like you promised to do. And I'll come back with some nice presents for the three of you. That I can promise."

Grandpa said, "Don't worry, Chuck. We'll have everything under control while you're gone. The tribes have been quiet as mice, ever since Judge Parker sentenced a bunch of 'em to be hanged. George Maledon can do twelve at a time on that new gallows of his, and sure enough he used it on a half dozen vicious half-breeds. Rapists and killers. I wish I could've been there to see 'em dangle."

Appalled by his salty language, Grandma Lucy said, "You shouldn't let the kids hear you talk like that, Jake!"

"Well," he told her, "facts is facts, and I ain't one to sugar-coat 'em."

Chuck said, "C'mon, Tommy, let's get goin'. We've got a schedule to keep."

Music to Tommy's ears. He climbed onto the seat of the buckboard on the passenger's side, his heart beating with anticipation.

3

Their horses laden with weapons and supplies, Heck Thomas and George Maledon left Fort Smith on their mission concerning the murder of John Garrett. It was hotter than the day before, and sweat was already staining their shirts and their wide-brimmed hats.

George said, "I'm gonna miss Johnny Garrett. He never let nobody scare him. He wasn't afraid of nothin'."

Heck said, "You know he was born a slave, don't you? When Lincoln freed 'em, he fought with that black regiment. Lots of 'em was killed by Jeff Davis's boys, of which I was one, and so were you."

"But I never killed any blacks," George said. "Lots of white blue-bellies, but no blacks, as luck would have it. Only because I never came across any. But if I had, I would've shot 'em for the sake of the Confederacy, which I looked upon as my country at the time, and I was damn serious about it."

Heck said, "But weren't you in the artillery? How would you've got close enough to see who your cannonballs and grape shot tore into and what color their skin was?"

"Seen 'em after they was dead or blown apart," said George, "and I never saw any black ones. I wasn't near where they was deployed."

Heck said, "I was only twelve years old when I joined the 35th Georgia Infantry as my uncle's courier. He was a colonel, and so was my uncle Henry. As a courier, I carried a Navy Colt, the Confederate imitation of it, so I could defend myself if a Union soldier tried to stop me, but that never happened. So I never shot nobody during the war, but I would've if I had had the chance, white or black."

"Don't blame ya," George said. "Like Sherman said, war is hell. I hate the son-of-a-bitch Northern general for what he did to Atlanta, but nonetheless he told the truth about war."

Heck said, "The freed blacks that fought for the North was determined to fight to the death 'cause they knew if they was captured they sure as hell was gonna be tortured. I'm not sayin' I condoned it, in fact I would've tried to stop it, even though I was only a boy, but I'm just stating it as a fact."

"Yeah, that it was," said George.

Conversation wasn't too easy while they were both riding in the stifling heat, with the clopping of their horse's hooves obscuring their words. So they both lapsed into their own thoughts, and since they were old men now, they had a tendency to look back on their lives, not so much with regrets but just with memories.

After the Civil War, Heck's father became the first city marshal of Atlanta, and Heck joined the city's police force at age seventeen. He was christened Henry Thomas, but he was extraordinarily feisty and rambunctious even as a child, and his daddy would say, "Give 'em heck, Henry!" And so he became known as Heck, and the Henry was dropped. When he was twenty-one he married his cousin, Isabelle Gray, the daughter of an Atlanta preacher, and during the course of their marriage they had five children. Even as a young father with family responsibilities, Heck would not balk at putting his life on the line, and he became known as a fearless gunfighter.

In 1875 he moved his family to Galveston and became a railroad guard for the Texas Express Company. His job was to put a stop to train robberies. In 1878 the Sam Bass gang tried to rob a train twelve miles east of Dallas. Heck was wounded in the shoot-out, but the gang got away with nothing because he had had the foresight to hide the cash in an unlit stove and put decoy packages in the safe. That maneuver got him promoted to chief agent.

He decided to form a posse to go after a pair of notorious murderers and cattle thieves, Jim and Pink Lee, who had been plaguing not just the white folks in Cooke County, Texas, but also the Chickasaw Nation. The Lee gang had ambushed a previous posse and killed four of its members, so the reward on them was up to $7,000. Heck and his men caught up with them in a hayfield and gave them a chance to surrender. But they answered with a barrage of rifle fire, and the end result of a two-hour shoot-out was that both bandits were killed and no posse members. The next day, there was a newspaper headline that read: *The Lee Brothers, the Most Notorious Desperadoes in Texas, go Down with Their Boots on!*

The publicity got Heck Thomas hired as a U.S. Deputy Marshal at Fort Smith in 1886, where he began working under Judge Isaac Parker. He soon became known as one of the best bounty hunters working the almost completely lawless Indian Territory. On his first sortie, he tracked down and arrested a bootlegger, a horse thief and eight murderers. Over the next few years, he usually worked singlehandedly and brought more outlaws to justice than anybody else working the Territory.

Teaming up with George Maledon to go after whoever had shot John Garrett was a notable exception to Heck's usually ironclad habit of working singlehanded. But they were both friends and colleagues of the murdered man, so Heck thought that George had the right to be involved. Anyhow, Judge Parker had ordered them to both take care of the problem. And, truth be told, Heck was fascinated with how Maledon could placidly hang men who were helplessly shackled and blindfolded, without letting it bother him. At least he shot them down while they were capable of fighting back, on a more or less equal basis. But he respected George because he didn't just hang people, he also had the guts to go out and hunt them and confront them while they were armed and dangerous.

Because of their long conversations at the Fort or on the trail, Heck knew that George was born in Germany and had migrated to Detroit with his parents when he was still a child.

When he grew up, he came to Fort Smith as an Arkansas police officer. And when the Civil War broke out he enlisted in the Arkansas Light Artillery. After the war was over, he went back to Fort Smith as a deputy sheriff, and in 1872 he was put in charge of the execution of condemned prisoners. As part of his job as a jailer, in addition to his work as hangman, he had shot five prisoners trying to escape, and had killed two of them.

Earlier in the year 1895, the deepest tragedy of his life befell George Maledon when his eighteen-year-old daughter, Annie, was murdered by a bootlegger named Frank Carver. Isaac Parker sentenced Carver to hang, and George Maledon was anxious to carry out the sentence, but a fancy lawyer appealed the case to the Arkansas Supreme Court, and it was commuted to life in prison.

George never got over what he thought of as a travesty of justice. He started accepting more assignments of tracking down murderers. And he'd rather shoot them than hang them. But he got satisfaction out of it, no matter which way it went down.

When they came to a pond where they could water their horses, George said, "I wonder if Pat Garrett mighta been Johnny's daddy. That last name ain't a common one, is it?"

Heck said, "If so, Pat would never admit it. If it came out he's got a black son, his fans would turn on him. He's ridin' his fame for shootin' Billy the Kid, and he don't need no scandal, even though he didn't do it the way it's shown in that New York play. They didn't draw on each other. Pat sneaked up on Billy in the dark and shot him when he was unarmed. Big hero!"

"I heard Johnny Garrett's mom was Cherokee," George said. "And his daddy was black."

Heck said, "Either way, his blood was the same color as ours, that's for damn sure. Nobody I ever shot had any other color but red."

"I'm gonna have to get used to tellin' whoppers, like Pat Garrett," George said. "That writer what interviewed me this mornin' said I'm gonna be the hero of a whole bunch of dime novels, just like Pat."

"Then you'll prob'ly pretend you don't know me no more," Heck told him.

4

As the horse-drawn buckboard traversed a broad flat plain with rocky buttes on both sides, Tommy worked up the nerve to ask his dad about yesterday's hanging. He said, "You didn't want me to see that kind of thing, but you didn't really want to see it either, right, Dad?"

"It's a gruesome practice, and no civilized nation should be doing it," Chuck said.

"But our preacher says an eye for an eye is in the Bible," Tommy said.

"It is in there, but that doesn't make it right," his dad said. "The Bible was right in its time, but we've gotten more enlightened and less bloodthirsty now. Or at least we should have."

All of a sudden there was a clatter of hooves from somewhere up ahead, and four riders appeared on the horizon as if out of nowhere, whooping like savages and firing rifles and pistols.

Tommy's dad grabbed for a rifle under the seat of the buckboard, but as he tried to whip it into firing position, a bullet struck him in the shoulder and the rifle dropped with a clatter.

Tommy yelled, "Daddy! Daddy!"

Tears ran down his cheeks as he saw blood pouring from his father's wound.

At the same time, the four riders surrounded the buckboard, galloping round and round, sneering and laughing.

Tommy was torn between wanting to help his father and wanting to try to grab his father's rifle, and he decided to go for the rifle, but one of the men on horseback got to it first and snatched it up, barking out a mocking kind of laughter.

Belatedly a fifth rider appeared, riding a mule. And one of the others yelled at him, "Hey, Sheriff! Dig some spurs into that damn mule, will ya?"

The man on the mule said, "Cain't. He'll stop dead. And when he halts the stubborn son-of-a-bitch won't move again even if I beat him bloody."

Another of the strange men said, "Well, I think we got your horse back for ya. Ain't he the one hitched to this buckboard?"

"Damned if he ain't!" said the man riding the mule and wearing a badge.

And one of the others laughed coarsely and said, "Well, well, well! We done caught us a horse thief!"

Tommy cried out, "My daddy is no horse thief, mister!"

This brought forth more brutish laughter from the five men. Two of them looked to be Indians, maybe from the Creek Nation. And the other three, including the one on the mule, were either black or a mixture of black and Indian. None of them looked older than in their late teens. They all had on neckerchiefs, wide-brimmed hats and high-topped boots. Their brown corduroy trousers were muddy, frayed and torn. Three of them wore old and tattered leather vests and the other two wore long, limp, leather coats that looked like hand-me-downs, including the one wearing a badge. Their pistols looked kind of junky, and their rifles had some of the bluing worn off. None of them were lever-action. They were the kind of weapons sold cheaply to Indians or poor whites. Nonetheless one of them had put a bullet into Chuck Palmer's shoulder.

Through his pain, Chuck managed to say, "That horse is mine, boys. I bought him five years ago at Fort Smith. Bought him at the livery stable, and I can prove it. I still have the bill of sale."

The five strangers just stared at him with sneers on their faces.

One of them said, "You got the bill of sale on you?"

"No, I don't carry it around with me," Chuck said. "All the other ranchers near my spread know the horse is mine, they seen me ride it to church. His name is Casey."

The one wearing the sheriff's badge said, "That horse is *mine!* His name ain't Casey, it's Blue Demon! And you stole him! Which is a hanging offense, right, guys?"

His four "guys" all snickered. Then they shook their heads in a falsely solemn way, like a form of mockery.

"Listen up, feller!" one of the black guys snapped. "You screwed up royally when you stole the sheriff's mount."

"That's my daddy's horse!" Tommy defended.

"Didn't your daddy teach you not to lie?" the black guy said.

Chuck said to the one wearing the badge, "How can you be a sheriff? You don't look no older than nineteen."

"You questioning my authority?" he shot back.

One of the Indians or half-breeds said, "He's older than he looks, mister. We're his posse, and we all been legally deputized by the Creek Nation. And just because we ain't white, we ain't about to take no crap from a lowdown horse thief!"

As he said this, he seized a rope hanging from the pommel of his saddle.

One of his companions said, "Let's have us a trial first. We cain't hang him without a fair trial, boys. That's what the law says, and we have to be law-abidin'. We gotta do what's right."

The one wearing the badge said, "Tie him up, and take that harness off of *my horse*. Blue Demon ain't *meant* to pull no wagon, he's a ridin' horse."

Chuck cried out, "Wait! I'm no horse rustler, I swear! You're makin' a big mistake!"

One of the half-breed-looking guys said, "That's what they *all* say. Right, Sheriff? How many men have we hanged, and they was all *innocent*—if we'd have listened to 'em, which we didn't."

The one with the badge said, "Damn straight, Maoma. Pure as the driven snow, to hear 'em tell it. But we could see right through their dirty *rotten lies!*"

The one referred to as Maoma said, "We wasn't born yesterday. Tell him, Sheriff."

Two of the self-proclaimed posse members got the horse unhitched from the buckboard while two others tied Chuck's hands and wrists with rope.

Their leader wearing the badge said, "We know he's guilty as charged, boys. So we can try him fair and square while the rope is around his neck and waitin' for him. Toss the noose over that low-hangin' limb over there and get him up on my horse."

Once again Tommy cried out. "That's *our* horse! His

name is *Casey*, and I gave him his name! My daddy let me name him on the day he was born!"

One of the half-breeds said, "So your daddy is a horse thief *and* a liar, and he taught *you* to lie, boy! What kinda upbringin' is that?"

"*You're* the big fat *liar!* Let my daddy *go!*"

Laughing mockingly at Tommy, they dragged his dad over to the tree and lifted him up onto the horse, then put the noose around his neck.

The one wearing the badge said, "We don't need no more testimony, we already heard *his* side of the story. Right, boys?"

Maoma said, "Yessir, Sheriff. We heard *both* sides, from the prosecution and the defense."

"So let's take a vote," said the one called the sheriff. "You boys'll be the jury, and I'll be the judge. By the authority that's vested in me, I hereby appoint you four men to the jury. Now that you've been chosen fair and square, how many of you are gonna rule that this here horse thief is guilty?"

They all piped up, one after another.

"Guilty as sin!"

"Aye!"

"Aye!"

"Amen!"

"Guilty as charged!" said the sheriff and self-appointed judge. "And I sentence you to death by hanging."

"*No!*" Tommy yelled desperately.

His dad said, "You're *crazy!* I didn't steal this horse! He's *not* yours! Please don't do this in front of my son!"

The self-appointed judge said, "I'm pledged to uphold justice, never mind my personal feelings. And I'll never dishonor my oath. Your son will learn by being a witness today that he must not stray from the straight and narrow. Right, boys?"

One of them said, "Right, Sheriff!" And they all burst into hearty guffaws.

Up on the horse and under the tree with the rope around his neck, Chuck begged, "Please don't hurt my son. He'll be all alone out here! Cherokees will get him. They like to adopt white boys and make them forget their folks."

The one called Maoma said, "What's so bad about that? Me and my brother Lewis is half Cherokee and half Negro. And the sheriff here is half Negro and half Creek. You sayin' there's somethin' *wrong* with that? I think that's what he's implyin', Rufus."

The one that Maoma addressed as Rufus was the one wearing the badge. He shook his head with fake overwrought sadness and said, "Maoma, this horse thief is incorrigible. Let's get on with his hangin'. Swift justice is true justice."

In utter anguish and despair, Chuck called out to Tommy, "Be a good boy, son! Take care of your Mommy! Tell her what happened to me! She'll know what to do!"

Rufus came over to Chuck and slapped the horse's rump, making it step forward, sliding out from under Chuck, letting him drop, jerk and swing.

Tommy jumped down from the buckboard and tried to run toward his father as he choked to death, but Maoma held him back. The young boy screamed and cried, but he couldn't get away.

Rufus said, "We'll let the kid have the buckboard to take his father home and bury him. We'll harness the mule to it. And I'll put the mule's saddle on Blue Demon."

Tears streaming down his face, Tommy cried, "His name is *Casey!* You *creep!*"

Suddenly there was a loud whoop and a burst of laughter from two of Rufus's pals, as they opened the hamper that was under the seat of the buckboard and saw how full of food it was.

One of them yelled, "We're gonna eat good, boys! There's ham sandwiches and even fried chicken and biscuits in here!"

5

As Heck Thomas and George Maledon rode across the flatlands of Arizona north of Fort Smith, they were surrounded by fields full of corn as far as the eye could see on both sides of the rutted dirt road. Farms had sprung up after a federally authorized land grab in 1893 of Cherokee land by white settlers.

After George and Heck watered their horses, ate cold baked beans and rolled and lit up some smokes, Heck said, "We don't dare ride into Cherokee Nation without a posse to back us up. Not if we don't wanna get skinned alive."

"Agreed," said Maledon.

The two lawmen were hated by the Indians even more than most other white people, because last year they had led the hunting down of Ned Christie, one of the Cherokee Nation's most revered heroes. Ned was born in a loosely scattered, impoverished community known as Rabbit Trap, and his early boyhood had been spent in his father's blacksmith shop where he not only learned how to forge horseshoes, knives and sickles but also became a skilled gunsmith. As he grew up, he became an astounding marksman with a rifle or pistol. His distrust of white people was deeply ingrained due to family stories of how his Irish grandmother had suffered and died on the Trail of Tears back in the 1830's. He harbored ingrained resentment against the blue-bellied soldiers whose predecessors had driven his tribe from their ancestral land in the southern United States and had marched them ragged and starving to an inhospitable place where the ones lucky enough to stay alive had to struggle to eke out a poverty-stricken existence.

During the Civil War, Ned's father, Watt Christie, sided with the Union, hoping to gain favor with Northern politicians. When the war ended, he got elected to the Cherokee legislature, a post he held for twenty years, then Ned succeeded him. Ned lived in Rabbit Trap with his third wife, Nancy, and his thirteen-year-old son, James. Although he had prestige among Cherokees, he was still as poor as other Indians, and to make ends meet and support an addiction to alcohol, he took to bootlegging.

One night he got falling-down drunk, and when he came out of his stupor his father told him that white men were coming for him because he was accused of killing a federal marshal named Dan Maples. He sent a message to Judge Isaac Parker that he would give himself up if the judge would grant him a chance to prove his innocence, but Parker refused. Ned vowed that he would rather die fighting than go to Parker's court to be hanged. He eluded apprehension for three years and got blamed for the murders of eleven men and a slew of stage holdups and bank robberies, which he may or may not have committed.

"Too many for one man to've done," said Heck Thomas.

"Couldn't have done 'em all," George Maledon agreed.

Back in of May of 1989 Heck and George were ordered by Judge Parker to go after Ned Christie and put an end to him once and for all. "I don't care if you bring him in dead or alive," Parker said. "The reward is up to a thousand dollars."

This was plenty of incentive for Heck and George. But looking back on it as they rested by the pond, Heck said, "I never thought he was guilty, I was just doin' my job."

"Yeah, try to get the Injuns to understand that," said Maledon.

The Cherokees bitterly maintained that Ned Christie had been innocent and had been railroaded by the white man's law. That is why no white lawmen were safe inside the Cherokee Nation, especially Heck Thomas and George Maledon. The Indians believed they must have tracked Ned Christie with the help of evil spirits, but in actuality it was a snitch, a renegade with a grudge, who had given them the tip.

They surrounded Christie with their posse after he had backtracked to his old home in Rabbit Trap.

Heck shouted, "United States Marshals! Come out with your hands up!"

But Christie poked his rifle through a shattered window and opened fire.

Heck yelled, "If you're gonna fight us, send out your women and children!"

But Christie kept firing, keeping the posse pinned down.

George Maledon sneaked around a corner of the house and set fire to it with a torch, hoping to smoke

Christie out. Nancy Christie ran out, and Heck ordered his men to hold their fire. "Send James out here, too!" he bellowed, but the thirteen-year-old boy stayed in the house with his father as the flames leapt and surged and black smoke swirled all around.

Christie opened fire again, and the posse started blasting.

Ned Christie's father showed up, and Heck asked him to try to get his son to surrender. "Tell him he'll be treated fairly," Heck said.

"I can see no evil in my son," Watt Christie said, "and I won't call him out here to be arrested and hanged. He's in the hands of the Great Spirit."

Stymied, Heck authorized two of the posse members to use dynamite. They sneaked up to the house with twelve sticks of it and lit the fuse. A terrific explosion blasted a hole in the house, and the posse poured rifle fire through the hole and through what remained of the windows. The fire raged fiercely, consuming the house— and when the roof fell in Ned Christie staggered out firing his Winchester like a crazy man, but his aim was off because he had taken shrapnel in his right eye. Through the smoke and fire his shots went wild. The posse riddled him with bullets, and when he fell Sam Maples, the son of the man that Ned had initially been accused of killing, ran up and emptied his revolver into Ned's body, making it jerk and twitch with every round, and if he wasn't dead before, he was dead then.

From up on a hill looking down at the carnage, a crowd of Indian women hugged each other and wept, trilling their song of mourning.

Ned Christie's body was displayed in a window of a dry goods store at Fort Smith, with his Winchester cradled in his dead arms, held in place by wires. His teenage son, James, was dead too; Heck and George had found his charred body in the house after the embers stopped smoking. Judge Parker praised the posse, and they shared in the reward, each man getting seventy-four dollars. Ned's father was allowed to claim his son's body, and he brought it back to Rabbit Trap to be buried in the family cemetery alongside of young James.

"It was such a sad way for him to end," Heck said to George. "He started out as an upstanding citizen. Then he got accused of murder, falsely if you ask me, and it set him on a downhill slide."

"A lot of these desperadoes have sad stories," George said. "And sometimes they even have a nugget of truth in 'em."

They chuckled wryly.

"Well, I hate to dampen your spirits," George said, "but how are we gonna carry this shit off?"

"Well, I ain't for gettin' our asses killed," Heck said. "What about we go see Peta Nocona before we do anything rash?"

"Great idea," said George. "He's a disgusting old bastard, but he always knows what's happening."

———

PETA NOCONA WAS plump and prosperous from selling herbs and potions to his tribesmen, and he lived in a fairly decent stucco house in a decrepit village called Dog Town, just outside of the reservation. He kept four or five young squaws in a group of teepees in a clearing adjacent to the house. None of them was over fifteen years old; he liked them very young. At age fifty or so, he had a seamed, leathery face, his gray hair hung in long braids, and he was wearing a string of turquoise beads, a braided leather belt with a big silver buckle, and a silk shirt printed with gaudy flowers.

Dismounting and tethering their horses at a hitching post near the house, George and Heck took a long look at a young squaw who was stirring a big cast-iron kettle over a sizeable fire. She stepped back while two others carefully fed in hides of raw leather for tanning in the liquid mixture, probably made from tree bark, which was steaming in the kettle. One of the squaws in a beaded dress and moccasins, like the others helping her, was a white girl, which wasn't easy for the two lawmen to discern because with her dark braids and darkly tanned skin she looked more like an Indian than otherwise. They assumed she had probably been a captive, but they knew that once captured children had lived with Indians for a while they usually didn't want to live among whites anymore, not even their original families.

Peta Nocona greeted Heck and George at the door to his house and invited them in, offering them goblets of wine, chunks of goat cheese and coarse, grainy bread.

Immediately showing them that he already knew why they were here, Peta said, "John Garrett was killed just down the road. Sit. Eat and drink. I will have his body brought to you."

The two lawmen didn't act startled; they knew that this Indian medicine man was inscrutable. "You know everything that happens around here," Heck said, popping a chunk of cheese into his mouth. "I'll surmise that you already know who killed him."

"I believe it was Rufus Buck and some others," Peta Nocona said in his laconic way. "The young Davis brothers and Sam Sampson and Maoma July. "They observed the hanging of Cherokee Bill yesterday at Fort

Smith, and it fired them with a rage that made them think they needed to kill somebody."

"Where are they now?" asked George Maledon.

Peta smiled a thin, inscrutable smile before he spoke.

"Who knows? But they won't get far. They won't know how to avoid capture or death. For they are all stupid."

"Stupid is the worst kind of dangerous," Heck said. "And now that they've gotten a taste of killing, they probably won't stop."

"If I were you, I would search south of here," said Peta Nocona. "They talked of heading toward Rabbit Town, where Ned Christie used to live. They idolize him and they wish to visit his grave. He is said to have killed eleven white people, and Rufus Buck bragged that he would beat that tally."

"Not if we stop him first," George Maledon said grimly.

"Good luck with that," said Peta Nocona. "But at the very least try to show some pity for Rufus's closest friends, Lewis and Lukey Davis. As children they were ripped away from their parents and treated wickedly by the nuns and priests who run the Indian school in Muskogee. I know, because the same things were done to me. They were beaten and sexually abused, and I was, too, when I was a child. They taught us that it was sinful to be pagans. They forced us to forget our rituals and our culture. We were forbidden to speak our birth language or practice our tribal ceremonies. They felt justified in beating us till we bled, because they thought they were doing God's work, driving heathen demons out of us. They cut each child's hair the same, like a bowl, so that we all looked like identical, miserable and pathetic urchins. If we tried to let our hair grow long again, they didn't give us any food. They were trying to make us grow up to look and act like the hated whites who had taken our land. Many of us died of white men's diseases like influenza and tuberculosis at that school, and they buried us without telling our mothers and fathers, who would never see us again."

"All right, that makes me feel awful about what you and the rest of 'em went through," George Maledon said. "But that don't justify turnin' yourself into a vicious murderer."

"My point is that they *didn't* turn themselves that way, they were *turned* by others," Peta said. "They called us dirty Indians. They called us children of the devil. And they murdered us not only culturally, but spiritually. Even if we survived physically, they made us become dead inside. I call it *Death by Civilization*."

"This happened to Rufus and the Davis boys?" Maledon said. "What about the other two?"

"Sam and Maoma are not bright. They are followers. They grew up poor, but with their birth parents. They think Rufus Buck is destined to become a great tribal leader and drive all the white people from our land. They don't know it is a false hope. Years ago, when Red Cloud was brought to Washington, D.C. to meet the Great White Father, his eyes were pried open, and he came back and told his people that the whites were as numerous as blades of grass on the prairie. He realized that we could not drive them away by terrorizing them, and he vowed that he would fight no more forever."

"He was tired of buttin' his head against a stone wall," said George Maledon. "If you can't beat 'em, join 'em. I wish you'd all learn to think like that so my job would be easier."

"Now you are talking like the nuns and the priests," Peta said sarcastically.

Heck said, "Tell me somethin', Peta. If you're so much kinder than white people, why do you live in this nice house but you keep your squaws are out there livin' in teepees?"

"They need to know and live their heritage."

"And you get to have as many of them as you want?" Maledon said. "To sleep with you? *All* of 'em? Even as young as they look?"

"Women are capable of birthing children when they start showing monthly blood at twelve or thirteen," Peta said. "It's a signal that they are ready, and it's nature's way, for a good reason. Younger females don't die in childbirth as often as older ones do. King Solomon, the most revered of the ancients in your Christian Bible, had many, many wives. I took that lesson to heart at the Indian school, among many other lessons, some of which the nuns did not suspect that I was learning while I was being abused and beaten."

"Well, polygamy is against the law," Heck said. "But George and I have got more important things to attend to at the moment. So you keep right on practicing your heritage till Judge Parker takes a notion to tell us to do somethin' about it."

"You told us your sad story about Rufus Buck and Lukey Davis," Maledon said. "But what about the other three? I suppose they've got their own sad stories to justify why they turned out that way."

Peta said, "I would say that they are products of the same overall abuse of *all* Indians by you white people. Our souls are implanted in soil that you have already made poisonous, like the rest of your civilization. As a result, we do not thrive, we grow up under a taint of underlying bitterness which is easily turned into a thirst for revenge. We are like chained dogs whipped and kicked from the time we are puppies, so we itch to turn on you and give you some of your same kind of treatment."

"Well, it's our job to make sure you don't get away with that," said Heck Thomas.

Peta said, "Goodbye for now, gentlemen. Some of my fellow tribesmen would kill me if they saw me talking with you. But my squaws won't speak, knowing I would cut their tongues out."

"Somehow I don't think you're kiddin' about that," Maledon said.

6

On their way toward Rabbit Town, George Maledon was on his horse, but Heck Thomas was leading his by the reins. John Garrett's dead body was tied face down over the saddle, so he had to walk.

Tired and miffed, he said, "I didn't say you could ride all the way, George. It's hot as hell, damn it! When in Christ's name do you expect to take *your* turn walkin'?"

"Let me ride a while longer. My lumbago is killin' me."

"I get tired hearin' it. Sometimes I think it's just an excuse."

"Well, I wouldn't wish this lumbago on a dog, not even you, Heck. It hurts like hell in the middle of my lower back, and when it gets really bad, like it is now, the pain goes all the way down my legs and into my feet."

"What do you do for it?"

"Lie on my back and rest, and use hot compresses. Whisky helps the most, though. It numbs the pain and relaxes the muscles."

"Now you're sayin' you got an excuse for drinkin'

whisky. The lumbago gets you out of work, or in this case out of having to walk, plus makes you feel good about gettin' drunk."

"I *always* feel good about gettin' drunk," George said.

"You don't seem to have no lumbago when you're posin' on top of that gallows platform like the lord god of justice. You enjoy your work too damn much, George."

"My lumbago *always* hurts—I just don't let on about it when I'm in the public eye. I'm mindful I've got a reputation to uphold, and I always make sure I do Judge Parker proud. That's why that reporter, Crosby, is gonna put me in the dime novels. Like Bill Cody."

"Buffalo Bill?"

"That's what they call him. He's puttin' on his Wild West Show next year in Cleveland. I'd like to go see it, maybe go by rail, I'm saddle sore enough, by God! How can Easterners think what we do out here is glamorous or somethin'?"

"You don't see any glamour in shootin' the bad guys full of holes?"

"Lotta glamour in the dime novels. Trumped-up glamour—but it sells, Heck. You oughta get some of that action for yourself. You got enough of a reputation."

"Too much of one," said Heck.

———

JUST A FEW MILES up the road, Tommy Palmer was lying face down at the edge of a stream, and he was gulping water.

He sat up, water soaking his face and shirt, and washed off the dried tears on his cheeks. The buckboard bearing his father's body was nearby, and the mule was held upright by the harness, preventing him from bending to get a drink, so Tommy filled his hat with water and brought it to the mule.

Suddenly Tommy's eyes went wide and he shuddered as he looked up at the sky.

Buzzards were circling, swooping downward in a spiral, threatening to land on his dad's dead body.

He hurriedly put his dripping-wet hat back on his head, jumped up onto the seat of the buckboard and jerked on the reins yelling, "Giddyup, mule! *Giddyup!*"

————

MEANWHILE, Heck and George were still plodding along the trail, and George was still the one riding.

Heck said, "I'd like to see that gal Annie Oakley, see if she's all she's cracked up to be. They call her Little Sure Shot. She's supposed to be able to shoot ten silver dollars right outta the sky before any of 'em land, but I damn sure don't believe it. Nobody can shoot like that, not even me, George."

"Me neither," said George. "Must be some kinda trick to it."

Heck said, "It's all showmanship and Bill Cody's got the handle on it. He puts on stagecoach holdups, bank robberies, the whole works. You don't do nothin' fancy like that, George. Since when do you get to be such a celebrity just for hangin' people?"

"Well, I'm not just a hangman, I'm a deputy marshal, don't forget, just like you. I've shot a few people, too, Heck. Not as many as you have, but at least half a dozen. I shot a couple of 'em when they was about to escape from Judge Parker's jail."

"Yeah, and they was unarmed, and you shot 'em in

the back. That's the *easy* way. Not like they was comin' at you head-on with their guns blastin'."

"Are you tryin' to tell me you never killed nobody from ambush? You can't say that with a straight face, Heck! And I ain't tryin' to—"

George broke off in the middle of a sentence, and he and Heck stopped in their tracks.

They had spied a mule-driven buckboard approaching on the trail in front of them, and they stared at it for a long moment.

Tommy Palmer spotted them at the same time. Terribly scared of who they might be and what they might do to him, Tommy pulled hard on the mule's reins. Then, as the buckboard lurched forward, he glanced back frantically at the bed of the wagon and saw his father's body sliding forward on its back and hitting head first into the back of the driver's seat, with the force of the sudden stop.

This was enough to make the boy's tears start flowing again.

The two men in the road were getting closer.

And Tommy just stared at them, not knowing what to do.

When they got close enough, they looked the boy over, then George Maledon said, "Hold up there, boy! What's goin' on here?"

Tommy shivered as he stared at the deputy marshal badges worn by Heck and George. He stammered, "Are y-y-you real sheriffs?"

Puzzled, the two lawmen looked at each other quizzically.

Maledon finally said, "Relax, boy, we ain't gonna arrest you."

Heck said, "We're federal marshals for Judge Parker,

out of Fort Smith. And we've got the badges to prove it, son."

Tommy said in a choked-up voice, "The man who hanged my daddy wore a badge, too. He called my daddy a horse thief. But I don't think he was a real sheriff."

Heck walked around the side of the buckboard, stared at the dead man lying face up in the bed, and took note of the rope burns on his neck.

He asked, "Is this your daddy, son?"

"The man with the sheriff badge let me take Daddy home to bury him."

"His badge said Sheriff, not Marshal?"

"Yessir. There was four men with him, and they said they were his deputies. But they all looked too young, and a couple of 'em were half-breeds."

Heck and George shot each other meaningful looks. Then Heck said, "Son, the dead man on my horse is Sheriff John Garrett. The ones you're talking about must've killed him, and one of them is wearing his badge."

"Rufus Buck," George Maledon pronounced. "Gotta be Rufus Buck and his gang. John Garrett would jump on their asses every chance he got, tryin' to keep 'em in line and hopin' they'd smarten up. He put Rufus in the slammer more'n once. Some of his cronies, too."

"They prob'ly think they can get away with damn near anything they want, now that Johnny is dead," Heck said. "That's prob'ly why they got rid of him."

Maledon said, "They was already suspected of some rapes and killings, but nobody could prove it."

Heck said, "We've gotta make sure this kid gets his daddy back home and buries him. We can't let him wander around out here by hisself."

7

On horseback, the Rufus Buck gang approached a clearing in the woods where there was a dinky little cabin with a tarpaper roof and a dilapidated chicken coop with a rooster and a few chickens pecking and squawking inside a rickety wire fence. Nailed to the weather-stained wall of the coop was a hand-scrawled sign on a piece of rain-wrinkled cardboard: FRESH EGGS 25 CENTS.

Rufus signaled the gang to dismount, and they tied their horses to the branches of a tree, then stood together in a bunch, scoping the place out.

Lukey Davis said, "We gonna just take what we want?"

Rufus said, "Damn right, Lukey, nothin's gonna stop us. But Bart don't keep the best stuff in plain sight. Not in his shack neither. He hides it in the coop, and Peta Nocona spilled the beans abut it once when he was damn near blind drunk. When he sobered up he prob'ly forgot he even opened his trap about it. He acts so fuckin' smart but he's a dumb fuck."

Rufus motioned for his guys to follow him, and they crept closer to the chicken coop. It had a couple of small windows, but they were too filthy and smeary to let anybody see in. Rufus made a throwing motion, and Maoma picked up a rock and threw it through it one of the grimy little windows—*crash!*

Bart Smith, a grizzled, unwashed old man, came running out of the coop with a basket full of eggs. When he saw Rufus and the others, he stopped short and half the eggs fell out and broke on the rocky soil. But he choked back his anger and tried to sound like he wasn't upset.

"You done made me break half my eggs, boys," he said half apologetically, and even managed a light chuckle.

Lukey said, "Pick 'em up and scramble 'em. We could sure use some breakfast."

Rufus said, "He's got some stuff we c'n use more'n that. Ain't that right, Bart?"

"Well, I surely don't mind givin' you boys a taste of my good whisky. I got plenty in the coop."

Rufus said, "What if we was to want it all? Would you be real nice to us? Or would we hafta beat your scrawny ass first?"

"No...no...you don't have to hurt me...but please don't take all of it. Leave some for my customers. I have to make a living, boys."

Lewis Davis said, "We don't give a shit about your customers."

And his brother Lukey said, "What about rifles? And Colt pistols? And lots of ammo?

That's what we really need, Mister Bart."

"Sure...sure...I can spare a couple rifles...and the

ammo to go with 'em. I guess you boys're fixin' to go huntin'. If not, I don't wanna know no different."

Maoma said, "Goin' huntin'. That'd be a good thing to tell anybody come lookin' for us, Mister Bart."

The whole gang laughed, but the laughs sounded more evil than jolly.

Bart used to think of these five mean and nasty teenagers as a bunch of dumb kids, but now it dawned on him that they had become more threatening than a nest of rattlesnakes. He used to be brash and nervy, but now he was old and fearful. He just wanted to live out the rest of his life without being maimed or crippled. He was more scared of what Rufus and his bunch might do to him than he used to be of lawmen's bullets when he ran with the Dalton gang. Bob and Grat Dalton had both been marshals alongside of Heck Thomas, but they turned to rustling and bank robbing, which Heck viewed as a personal betrayal. He was hot on their trail in 1892 and almost caught up with them before they were gunned down in Coffeeville, Kansas, trying to rob two banks at one time to get enough cash to run away to South America.

Bart had been a lookout for the Daltons on some of their robberies, but had never appeared on a wanted poster. Out of fear of heck Thomas and his posse, he had chickened out of the Coffeeville thing, which had then turned into a fiasco. Bob and Grat got shot full of holes by up-in-arms townspeople who took umbrage over them trying to rob the two town banks where most of them had their money.

Bart turned over a new leaf, not by going straight, but by turning his attention to the safer enterprise of selling black-market liquor and stolen guns. He always kept his merchandise well hidden and trusted almost nobody. The "almost" in the case of Peta Nocona now had him scared that he was going to die today.

Trying to curry favor by telling Rufus something he might not know, he said, "Heck Thomas is after you boys, him and that hangman, George Maledon. I heard about it from Peta Nocona. He was here buyin' whisky. They think you killed that sheriff, Johnny Garrett, who used to put you boys in the clink now and then. They figure that was your motive."

"Well, they're fulla shit," Rufus said. "Sounds like maybe John Garrett got what was comin' to him. Lotsa folks wanted him dead, not just us. We better not find out you was tellin' stories on us, Bart."

"C'mon now, Rufus, I know how to keep my mouth shut," Bart said. "But I know what I know. Them two lawmen showed up at Peta Nocona's place, and he had some of his people fetch Sheriff Garrett's body to 'em. I don't know why he was doin' 'em the favor. I got no love for Heck Thomas—not for George Maledon neither!"

"What you got against 'em, old man?" Rufus said snidely, as if Bart was too old and inept to matter.

"You're gonna get old yourself someday, if you live long enough. I wasn't always an old man."

With a fake smile on his face, Rufus said, "We're real sorry about your broken window, Mister Bart. Maoma was aimin' to hit a cat that was prowlin' on the roof of your chicken coop, but he missed and hit the window. The cat skedaddled. You ain't mad at us, are ya?"

"Oh no...no...not at all, boys. Wait right here and I'll bring you a bottle of firewater from under the straw."

"Don't call it firewater, goddamn it!" Rufus snapped. "That's what you call it when you water it down and sell it to Injuns. You get 'em drunk, then fleece 'em."

"Now be fair to me," Bart said pleadingly. "Many's

the time I give your father eggs for free, Rufus. You remember that, don't ya?"

"Sure, I remember. I remember how you charged us triple price for a chicken, then tossed in a couple old smelly eggs you couldn't sell to the whites that gave us trinkets and candy so's they could steal our land. But we ain't gonna stand for it anymore. We're gonna rise up and drive 'em out. But we need better guns than what we got."

Bart said, "You can't scare all the whites off by butcherin' and scalpin'. We've all got to learn to git along, Injuns and white men...and even blacks. I don't mean no offense, mind. I like you boys, even the ones who are dark."

Maoma said, "Shut up and fetch that whisky, old man! Don't be stingy now. Bring a bottle for each of us."

"Sure...sure...I don't mind. I hide my best stuff in the coop. Wait right here...I'll bring it out."

Rufus and his boys gave each other sly looks as Bart went into the chicken coop.

He brushed a covering of straw from a case of brand-new lever-action Winchesters. He looked all around, then hurriedly dumped out a box of cartridges and started loading them into one of the rifles with straw still clinging to it.

But Lukey barged in and caught him at it—and gunned him down right then and there. Four slugs thudded into Bart's frail body, knocking him off his feet and onto the ground, gushing blood and setting all the hens to squawking and flapping.

Lukey giggled and licked his lips as Rufus and Maoma stepped into the coop and laughed when they saw Bart give a final kick of his left foot as the breath wheezed out of him and he died.

Rufus said, "First we'll help ourselves to a bunch of rifles and ammo. There should be Colt .45s socked away in here, too, 'cause I got drunk with a white man who had one and he tol' me where he got it."

Lukey said, "We could sell rifles and pistols for a lot of cash, Rufus."

"Damn right, but we ain't gonna sell 'em. Let's get hold of that whisky and have us a hell of a party. Then we'll raise so much hell in this Territory that us'ns'll go down in history. We'll make the Daltons and the Youngers look like choir boys."

8

It was dusk by the time Heck Thomas and George Maledon got to the ranch house where Tommy Palmer had lived with his father, mother and grandparents. Tommy was still driving the buckboard with his dad's body in back. George was now leading horse bearing John Garrett's dead body and Heck was taking his turn riding the other horse.

Dismounting, the two lawmen motioned Tommy to stop the buckboard and stay back while they moved in close and crept up onto the front porch with their guns drawn.

Heck went in first, with George right behind him.

The first thing they saw was the dead body of Tommy's grandfather, Jake Warner, hanging from the rafters of the front room. His purple tongue was lolling out and two kitchen knives were sticking out of his torso. His hands were cut off and lying pale and claw-like in a puddle of blood on the floor underneath him.

Frozen in place, Heck and George swept their eyes around the room in the dim light, and saw that Tommy's grandmother, Lucy Warner, had suffered a horrible death. She was sagging upright against a plank wall, held there by big nails driven into her wrists and hands. Her dress had been ripped open, her breasts had been hacked off, and her pale chest was a red, pulpy mass of mangled flesh.

Lying near her, on the floor face up, was the dead body of Tommy's mother, Clara, in a huge pool of sticky-looking blood. Her neck had been slit almost to the point of decapitation. Her dress was pulled up around her waist and the top of it was ripped open, exposing her pale breasts and pink nipples.

Suddenly a *scream*. The two lawmen wheeled around and saw that Tommy hadn't stayed back like he was told, but had crossed the threshold a few feet behind them and had seen it all—all the death and torture.

George grabbed him in a hug and forced him back out, and tears were streaming down the boy's face. He started choking out words, between his sobs.

"Jolene...Jolene...my sister. Where is she? They must've took her..."

Maledon said, "Easy, boy, we don't know that yet."

Tommy screamed, "I'll kill 'em! I'll *kill* 'em! Let me *go!*"

Heck came out onto the porch and said, "Calm the boy down if you can, George. I wanna look around some. Down by the barn."

He pointed up at the sky so George would see the buzzards circling above the area of the barn. Then he drew his gun and moved off slowly but purposefully, and when he got there he crept inside and prowled around, then climbed a ladder high enough to peer into the loft, but found nothing and no one. Just straw and empty stalls.

He came back out and crept around the side of the barn, pistol at the ready.

Then he stopped with a sudden jerk.

He had stumbled upon a dead body, flat on its back, with a pitchfork sticking straight up out of its chest. A buzzard had already landed on it, and more of them were circling down, coming closer.

Heck turned away and headed back toward the ranch house. He saw that George was still hugging Tommy and patting him, trying futilely to comfort him.

He holstered his pistol because there was nobody to shoot at. The bad guys had probably been here while he and George had been poking along with a dead body on a horse and another one in a mule-driven buckboard. It was the Rufus Buck gang all right. He had recognized Maoma July. He knew Maoma from previous arrests and Maoma had been mentioned as one of the gang members by Peta Nocona.

9

George and Heck took picks and shovels from the barn and dug a hole deep enough to bury Chuck Palmer and the members of Tommy's family who were tortured and murdered at the ranch. They let Tommy toss in some dirt and take the lead saying some prayers, crying his eyes out and shaking all over.

They dragged Maoma July's body onto the buckboard to take it to Fort Smith and collect any reward money that might be on him, and agreed that they should give the money to Jolene Palmer if she should ever be found. Then they unhitched the mule and put it in the barn and harnessed Heck's horse to pull the wagon while George rode his own horse back to Fort Smith. Tommy rode on the seat of the buckboard with Heck, and Heck took up the reins.

They got to Fort Smith a couple hours after nightfall and took Tommy to stay with his paternal grandparents, who had to endure the sudden shock of learning about all the deaths that had taken place at the ranch house. They broke down, hugging Tommy, sobbing and moaning, and this was without yet hearing anything about the torture and the rape. George and Heck felt that there would be time enough for them to have to deal with the ugly details, and therefore, at that moment, the lawmen had no appetite for getting into it. Not with Tommy there, in any case. He had already seen all the horror up close and personal, by accident, because they had not blocked him from stepping across the threshold. Maybe he would spill it all, or pieces of it, before the grandparents got him comforted enough to put him to bed.

———

HECK WENT to his house outside of the fort, where he knew that his wife would be up worrying about him. He had been divorced once and didn't want it to happen again. He was trying to be a more dutiful and attentive husband this time around. Several years back, when he was constantly hunting down and bringing dozens of outlaws to justice, his first wife, Isabelle, had gotten so fed up with the constant danger on the frontier and her husband's long, lonely absences that she abruptly moved back to Georgia, taking their five children with her. Heck was so devastated by the divorce that he desperately did not want to lose another marriage. His second wife, Mattie, was a schoolmarm and preacher's daughter who had nursed him back to health in 1889 after he got wounded in a shoot-out in Oklahoma. They fell in love while he was recovering under her care, and got married a year later.

She was four months pregnant and wasn't showing it very much when she fell into his arms as soon as he came through the front door, back from chasing the Rufus Buck gang, so far without the kind of success that he wanted. He told her about it, toning down the gory details, while she put coffee on and warmed up some roast beef with gravy and mashed potatoes. It was late for such a heavy meal, but he wolfed it down and hoped that when he finally got into their bed, it wouldn't wake him up in the wee hours, with heartburn.

The world knew him as a relentless pursuer and killer of bad men, but she knew the tender side of him. They understood each other on a profound level. He knew she would always be there for him and that she would not stop him from being everything that he wanted to be. She accepted him and didn't try to change him, in spite of her worries.

She was a small, well-kept woman, fifteen years younger than he was, no gray in her brown hair yet, at least none that was showing. Looking at her across the kitchen table, he was once again struck by the liveliness in her brown eyes and the kindliness in her face.

With subdued anxiousness, she asked, "Will you go out after them again?"

He nodded, chewing roast beef, then taking a sip of black coffee.

"How soon?"

"Pretty quick, I imagine. Those crazy fools aren't going to stop, and word of their next atrocity will come back to us."

"Oh, dear," she said, with a small sigh, eyeing him with affection and consternation.

She was a habitual caregiver, and regularly brought home-cooked food to some of the prisoners at the jail. He wished she wouldn't do it. He shuddered to think about the various escape attempts that had taken place, some of them successful. His major concern was that she might be hurt or taken hostage. But she thought that the culprits deserved an occasional break from their normal diet of stale bread, soggy scrambled eggs or cold baked beans and tepid water.

She said, "I know who Rufus Buck is, Heck. I tried talking to him one day when our preacher led a mission to Rabbit Town."

This took Heck aback. "Are you sure, Mattie? You were that close to him? Could it have been someone else?"

"No, I wouldn't forget that name. He was like a wild buck. He harbored a sullen anger deep inside of him just waiting to explode. I could tell. He was like a caged animal who would tear you apart if he ever got out."

"You're not ever going back there again, are you, Mattie?" Heck said it pleadingly. He didn't want anything bad to happen to her or their unborn child.

"I don't think so," she said.

But he could tell that her sense of Christian duty might someday cause her to take more risks.

"At least hold off till we get that damned gang captured," he said to her.

She said, "I can promise you that, I suppose. I'm foolish enough to believe there's some good in everybody. But I also have a deep sense of caution."

"Thank goodness for that," Heck said, hoping he could believe it.

———

GEORGE MALEDON ENVIED Heck because ever since his only daughter had been brutalized and killed by her husband, the hangman had no family of his own. He took pride in his work, but most women shied away from him when they became aware of what he did for a

living, so he believed that bachelorhood would be his
fate for the remainder of his life. One night when he was
drowning his sorrows in beer and bourbon, a smartass in
the saloon had mockingly called him "the Prince of
Hangmen" over and over again, till he got fed up and
took a swing at the guy. He was in no condition for a fist
fight, so he got his ass kicked. They got arrested for
brawling and disturbing the peace and would've been
thrown in the clink if Judge Parker hadn't let them go
with just a stern warning, without fining either one of
them. Looking back on it, George had to smile at his
remembrance of the judge showing him a touch of
mercy. Isaac Parker didn't like being called the Hanging
Judge any more than George Maledon liked being called
the Prince of Hangmen.

When Heck went home to his wife, George went to
the judge's house and knocked on the door even though
it was very late. Judge Parker was in slippers and a white
robe, and he said, "Let's not talk here, let's go to my
chambers." He puffed on a Meerschaum pipe while
George gave him a report about the horrible carnage at
the Palmer ranch house. After listening to it all with
silent attentiveness, and blanching now and then over
some of the worst details, the judge said, "Where's the
boy now?"

"Tommy's grandparents on his dad's side live right
here in town," George said. "We took him there. I sorta
know his grandpa and grandma, they run a drugstore."

The judge said, "Oh, yeah, I know them, too. Pretty
near everybody does."

George said, "I don't know what I woulda done with
the boy if his grandparents weren't handy. They're in
shock, overwhelmed with grief. I had to pound on their
door in the middle of the night. Me and Heck dug graves

for the folks we found at the ranch, and for Tommy's father, who had been lynched by those bastards. An awful job on him, too—his neck was cut into real deep by the rope."

Ignoring George's criticism of the way that someone else carried out a hanging, Judge Parker said, "They wanted to steal Chuck Palmer's horse?"

"Mostly they wanted to kill somebody," George said. "Had fun doin' it, too, the way Tommy told it. You ask me, they're the most diabolical crew that's ever been on the loose in Arizona Territory—and that's sayin' a lot. I'm gonna relish dealin' with 'em my way once they're caught and you sentence 'em. Their necks'll stretch before my ropes do. I keep 'em well oiled."

The judge said, "Well, at least there's one of them we won't have to worry about anymore."

"Maoma July. He's the one Heck found with a pitch-fork stickin' outta him. Someone in the Palmer family must've been fightin' him to get away and got him with the pitchfork."

"Do you think it could've been the daughter?"

"Coulda been her. Her name is Jolene, and she's only fourteen. Looks like they took her, maybe gonna hold her for ransom, let's hope, instead of rapin' and killin' her. Tommy says she woulda fought like hell. It woulda taken a lot of force to kill Maoma July that way, but even a young gal might've had the strength if she was fightin' for her life."

Judge Parker took another puff on his pipe and mulled things over. He said, "Heck's going to need backup when he goes back out. In fact he's gonna need a whole posse."

George agreed. "Yep, that's for sure, Judge. There was five of 'em, that's what Tommy told us, and so did Peta

Nocona, the lecherous old bastard. Then findin' Maoma July with that pitchfork in him cinched it. Heck wants to try to save Jolene before the worst happens to her. But we can't let him go up against those desperadoes all by hisself."

"He's a stubborn man, and I imagine he tells himself he shouldn't be overly scared of them because they're not even grown men yet, they're all teenagers."

"Yep, he says they're scarcely out of their diapers. But I told him it don't take an adult to pull a trigger."

"I suppose he has a plan. It'd be unlike him if he didn't."

"Well, he's all fired up and determined to try and save Jolene. But common sense tells me it's already too late."

"I suppose so," said Judge Parker. "But I pray not."

10

T*he Daily News Record*, one of several newspapers published in Fort Smith, Arkansas, covered not only the known atrocities committed by the Rufus Buck gang, but also some that were suspected but not proven. The horrendous spree of torture, rape and murder unleashed at the Palmer and Warner ranch was a staple of blaring headlines and bylines in the days following the rescue of ten-year-old Tommy Palmer and the disappearance of his sister Jolene.

The boy's grandparents thought it would be best for him not to hide in the house all the time, but to go out into the town as much as possible and try to do things that would be considered normal, in hopes that he would eventually be distracted enough that his suffering would ease. They didn't totally believe they were doing the right thing, but they didn't know how else to cope.

Both grandparents, Ezra and Elizabeth Palmer, ran their drugstore together. Ezra was the pharmacist, and Elizabeth, called Beth by her husband and her friends, was the clerk, the cashier and the manager of inventory

—in other words she stocked the shelves. They told Tommy that they wanted him to help at the drugstore because they had been about to hire another boy, but they couldn't afford to pay two. This was a bit of a fib. Their main motive was to make Tommy feel needed and also get him out of the house and among kindly people. They believed that otherwise he would stay bereft and locked inside himself. They were having a terrible time handling their own grief, as adults who had lost their in-laws and their only son, and they could only imagine how hard it must be for a ten-year-old boy. They paid him fifty cents a week for doing chores at the drugstore and at home, which they thought was only fair, and might help ease his pain.

But a twelve-year-old neighborhood bully picked on Tommy right in the main street of town, pushed him down in the dirt, and took the first half-dollar that Grandpa Palmer paid him. The boy was named Brucie Jenkins, the son of an alcoholic mother and a ne'er-do-well father who had deserted them both when Brucie was only three.

With Tommy hurt and lying in the dirt, Brucie said, "You tell anybody I took your half dollar, I'll tell everybody your sister is fuckin' Injuns."

Tommy didn't tell anybody. Instead he crept up behind Brucie in an alley the next day, and clobbered him in the head with a garbage can lid. Brucie bit the dust, shook his head groggily, and didn't get up right away. Tommy stood over him, still holding the garbage can lid, and said, "Gimme my fifty cents back or I'll hit you again."

Brucie reached in his pocket and tossed the half-dollar in the dirt, at Tommy's feet.

Tommy picked it up and pocketed it, then turned and

walked out of the alley.

When he turned onto Main Street, he spied a small crowd gathered in front of a place with a sign that said MORTUARY. He shuffled down the dusty street and found out that the people were gathered in front of a large plate glass window, so many of them that they were blocking his view of what they were gawking at.

Then he heard some high-pitched shouts and spun around to see three boys hurrying his way. They were wearing knickers and slouch hats and one of them was pushing a hoop with a stick. He stopped the hoop and held it upright as they got close to the mortuary.

Then several of the adult gawkers turned away from the window, leaving a gap through which the boys could see. The gawkers faced toward the boys, mumbling and shaking their heads. One of them said, "You young boys shouldn't be here."

The boy with the hoop said, "We wanna see, Mister!"

The man said, "Well, have a good look, then, and see what'll happen to you if you turn bad."

One of the other boys said, "Our teacher says we're *already* bad!"

Another man said, "Well, not as bad as this half-breed here. Just make sure you boys don't end up like him."

Tommy peered over the other boys' shoulders—and he suppressed a shudder when he saw Maoma July embalmed and put on display. He was propped up on a tilted board, and the pitchfork that killed him was leaning prongs up across his chest.

The three other boys stared at him, wide-eyed, and one of them giggled.

Tommy hoped it really was his sister's efforts that had caused the outlaw to end up as a display in the mortuary window.

11

Rufus Buck found his seventeen-year-old cousin, Charles Buck, fishing in a stream that they both used to frequent. Rufus was riding alone. He and his guys had temporarily split up and scattered after what they called "raids" on the Palmer ranch and on Bart Smith's black-market hideaway; tomorrow they were going to team up again at a preordained time and place in order to carry out their next escapade.

As Rufus rode up, on the horse taken from Chuck Palmer, he startled Charles for a moment, but when Charles saw who it was, he relaxed and tossed his trout line into the water. The place where the line went in shimmered and sparkled in the hot August sun, and Charles took his wide-brimmed hat off and wiped his sweaty forehead with the back of his hand. His skin was blacker than Rufus's and the sweat droplets glistened.

Rufus said, "Hello, there, cousin! Fishing is good?"

"So far I haven't caught anything. One bite, and I lost it. How are you, Rufus?"

"Fine and dandy. How are you, Charles?"

"Disgusted. My ma and pa want me to stay in the Indian school, but I don't want to. But they won't let me drop out. They say I have to learn to be like the whites now because our way of life is over."

Rufus shook his head disgustedly. "Why would they think like that? They know what the Indian school did to my mother. She calls it the Sister School."

"I know," Charles said with a grimace.

Growing up not just as cousins but as playmates, Charles often slept over at Rufus's house, a cabin without running water or an indoor toilet, just an outhouse. There was a pond to bathe in, which was okay in spring and summer, but in winter the ice was sometimes too thick to chip a hole in it. In spite of their poverty, the growing boys liked playing rough-and-tumble games together and talking and laughing till the wee hours at night, rolled up in blankets on the hard clay floor.

Charles adored Martisse, his aunt and Rufus's mother, who always treated both boys equally. He and Rufus had both observed her having "spells" and pacing back and forth for hours, trying to outrun her invisible demons. She would shake her head from side to side, flapping and wringing her hands as if her memories were evil spirits that she had to exorcise. When she wore herself out, she would cry, "Settle down, you crazy old chicken!" She would flop onto her straw mattress and cry and cry, trembling and trembling, till she fell asleep at last, and in the morning the mattress would be soaked with her tears.

One night when Charles wasn't there Rufus crawled into bed with his mother, cuddling as close to her as he could, and his hand touched a tiny Virgin Mary medal pinned to the top of her nightgown. He realized that she must have kept it from her hateful boarding school days. Her bedspread was stiff from her dried tears. She would spend hours and hours washing the sheets like the Sisters had taught her, muttering "white, white" to herself over and over, struggling in and out of the house with baskets of wet, heavy bedclothes. "We may be Indian but by God we ain't dirty," she'd say while hanging the sheets on the line whether or not the sun was shining.

Rufus hated the whites and what their school did to his mother. And he knew that

Charles felt the same way. That is why he felt he could tell Charles the truth about what he had been doing. "I've started robbing whites and killing them," he boldly admitted. "To scare them off of this land. We're even raping their women, like they did to ours."

Charles's eyes widened, but he wasn't surprised or angry. He asked, "Who's this 'we', Rufus?"

"Me and our friends. Lukey, Lewis and Sam."

"What about Maoma?"

"A fourteen-year-old girl killed him while we were kidnapping her. He thought she was too young to hurt him, and he got careless. She didn't get away from us, though. We're gonna sell her for a lot of money."

"Sounds good to me," Charles said. "Want me to take Maoma's place?"

"That's what I was about to ask you."

"Fuck the Indian school," Charles said, and he pulled his trout line out of the water.

12

On the same day that Rufus Buck recruited his cousin Charles Buck to take Maoma July's place as a gang member, Sheriff John Garrett's funeral took place at Fort Smith. The funeral cortege, led by a black horse-drawn hearse, paraded down the wide main street of town. It was a dirt street but the dirt was packed down level and hard to keep dust or muddy ruts to a minimum. Thriving businesses lined both sides of the street, and dozens of people came out of the shops to watch the procession.

Heck Thomas and George Maledon were marching along with the crowd of mourners behind the hearse, and they saw Tommy Palmer come out of his grandparents' drugstore with a dust rag in his hand. The boy took a long, awestruck look at what was going on, then abruptly turned around and hurried back inside.

"Was that Tommy?" Heck said.

"Yeah," said George. "Almost didn't know him with that hat pulled down and the knickers on him. I guess his grandpap and grandma gave him somethin' to do to keep his mind offa things."

"Good idea," said Heck. "I worry about how he's gonna get on, with all he's been through. It'd be enough to floor an adult."

"I think he'll do okay with the passing of time," George said. "He's got a lot of spunk."

"It'd help if we could find his sister and reunite them," Heck said.

The funeral procession proceeded to the Mount Jordan Baptist Church on one of the side streets in the poor section of town, which was packed with several hundred mourners, plus a raft of others lining the street and sidewalks. The congregation was mostly black, but for the service today lots of white people and Indians had come to pay homage to Sheriff John because of his bravery in trying to bring law and order to a mostly lawless territory.

John's wife and three children were in a pew up close to the coffin and they couldn't stop crying. The eulogy lasted for over an hour and was rife with wholesale sobbing and singing, and afterwards, like everyone else, Heck and George felt drained and deeply saddened.

"Gotta wet my tonsils after that ordeal," Heck said.

"Me, too," George said. "That's for damn sure. We paid our respects and did what we could for the time being, but our real tribute to John Garrett will occur when we bring his killers to justice."

"Hopefully at the end of a rope," Heck said.

They ambled to the Fort Smith Saloon to discuss strategies for tracking the gang down. They were served quickly because of their badges and their familiarity with the bartender and waitresses, and soon they had shot glasses, tin cups, a bucket of beer and a bottle of bourbon brought to their round oaken table, where they were sitting in a corner by themselves.

The saloon was dark and smoky, lit by hanging lanterns putting out kerosene smoke to mix with cigarette and cigar smoke. There was a gaudy portrait of a plump naked lady behind the bar, sawdust on the plank floor and a shiny spittoon a few feet from the table, but neither man was smoking or chewing.

First thing they did was clink shot glasses and toss down slugs of bourbon followed by beer chasers. They didn't get down to their immediate concerns right away, but instead chatted about fugitives from the law that they could've been going after if they weren't preoccupied by the atrocities of the Rufus Buck crew.

Tom Horn was one of the most widely feared gunslingers of the day, a once respected army scout, prospector and rancher, who had been driven into bankruptcy by a gang of rustlers who stole his herd of cattle and burned his ranch house down. It made him so bitter that he felt justified in becoming a hired killer. He felt immune to punishment and even bragged in a newspaper interview, "If a fellow's killing can be justified as authorized and legal, by means of getting myself deputized to go after him, I first give him a warning, then I shoot him down without a shred of remorse."

"He's lookin' to become a customer of mine," George said, taking a sip of beer.

Heck grinned, then shook his head. "He got hisself more famous than ever when he took part in Geronimo's surrender in '85. How things do change, George. That was only ten years ago when he was on the top of the world. Now he's killin' rustlers for the big cattle companies, and they protect him from prosecution."

"He even has a trademark," George said. "Shoots 'em

from a hiding place, then goes down and rolls 'em over to make sure they're dead, then puts a little pebble under their heads."

"Shows the rest of 'em he's in the area so they'll run to someplace else. By now they're so damn scared of him, all he has to do is ride around and let people see him, and the thieving stops for a while."

"Sometimes he makes people disappear. Nobody knows where. But it's pretty clear he musta killed 'em."

Heck said, "He only does that if there's no bounty on them. If there's a bounty, he's got to show the bodies so he can collect."

"There was two guys early this year that everybody knows he killed, and he got brought in but was never charged. It's an open secret that he's a hired gun for the Wyoming Stock Growers Association, and they must have put a lot of money in the right hands to get that case dismissed."

"Well, these are rough and tumble times for sure, George. It all started happening when cattle ranchers started usin' barbed wire to fence off their land and their water rights. And startin' wars against the sheep ranchers."

"Yeah, they lynched and burned the corpses of two sheep guys last year, and not a damn thing was done about it."

"Makes me wanna just get drunk and cry myself to sleep," Heck joked, and tossed down another shot.

"We're livin' in a dog eat dog world out here," George said grimly.

"Well, you gotta choose sides," Heck said. "And you and me chose right. Tom Horn's gonna push his luck too far and end up shot dead or on the wrong end of a rope."

"Well, sad to say, I won't get to do the honors," George said, " if he gets arrested over there in Wyoming. But he's done some dirty deeds in Arkansas, too, so he might come under this jurisdiction, and Judge Parker'll be waitin' for him."

Heck said, "I hope he stays in Wyoming. We got plenty enough problems on our plate, and Tom Horn is a lot smarter and sneakier than the ones we're dealin' with."

George tossed down a shot glass of bourbon, smacked his lips and waited for the throat burn to subside. Then he said, "Stupid fuckers are harder to catch than smart fellers 'cause they do shit without any rhyme or reason. Hard to get a handle on what they might do next or where they might be headed. Too unpredictable."

"Normally we'd have tracked 'em from the Palmer place," Heck said. "But we had the boy to take care of. Now we gotta catch up to 'em somehow, and they could be just about anywhere either near or far from here."

George grimaced musingly and said, "Only thing I can think of is, we go back out there and try to pick up a cold trail. There was lots of tracks. We've gotta try to follow them."

"I don't think they got a pile of loot," Heck said. "They didn't even ransack the place, prob'ly realized all their victims was too poor. Rape and murder was all that was on their fucked-up minds."

"And taking that young girl with 'em," said George. "Why didn't they rape and kill her right there?"

"Maybe they wanna keep her for a sex slave," Heck speculated. "They're a bunch of perverts, we know that for *damn* sure."

George said, "If they had gotten a load of cash, they'd

already be in a bar somewhere raisin' hell and callin' attention to themselves."

"Gotta hope they do somethin' that tells us where they are," Heck agreed. "Trouble is, lots of folks'll prob'ly die and that's how we'll be able to close in on 'em again."

13

The sign said U.S. ARMY TRADING POST. It was a big, clean-looking log building with white plaster smoothly laid in, between the fat brown logs. Two sentries in blue uniforms with yellow-striped trousers stood guard on each side of the building on an expansive plank porch with hitching posts out front. Several saddle-horses were tethered there, along with a couple of wagons with horses in harness.

Holding the reins of their horses as they hid among trees and tall weeds on the other side of the dirt road, Rufus Buck and Lewis Davis eyed the trading post, armed with spanking new rifles and pistols stolen from Bart Smith.

Charles Buck, the young fledgling member of the gang, remained on a horse that had a travois lashed to it. And on the travois, gagged and bound with coils of rope, was Tommy Palmer's fourteen-year-old sister Jolene, her clothes ripped and gashed and her face smeared with blood.

Lewis Davis leaned in close to her, still holding the

reins of his horse, and spoke to her in a harsh whisper. "You best lie still and not make any noise, bitch. You give us away, I'll kill you. You remind me of how I wanna make you suffer every time I see Maoma's blood on your snotty face."

Rufus came over to Lewis and Charles as they stood by the travois. He cautioned them, "Be cool, and don't lose your nerve." He meant this for Charles more than Lewis, since this was going to be his young cousin's first ambush.

The previous evening, as he and Charles sat around a campfire and smoked peyote in the blackness of a cloud-filled night, Rufus got Charles's anger stoked to a raging fire by telling him the story of the Wounded Knee Massacre, where peaceful Sioux Indians were attacked without warning and over 150 women and children were butchered by the 7th U.S. Cavalry, which was re-consti-tuted after the deaths of General Custer and his men at Little Big Horn in 1876. "We killed the blue-bellies fair and square," Rufus said to Charles. "But the cowards let fourteen years go by till they took their revenge on our squaws and our children."

"Where were the warriors?" Charles asked innocently.

"They were doing the Ghost Dance. It was supposed to make them invisible and immune to bullets. They believed a medicine man who told them this, because they wanted to believe it. He told them that when the whites were all dead, the ghosts of the buffalo would all come alive and populate the plains by the thousands, just like it used to be."

"That sounds dumb," said Charles.

"Well, they were desperate enough not to see through it," Rufus told him. "We have to kill the whites, but we can't expect the buffalo to come back anymore. All we can hope for is that the whites will leave our land and we will have it all to ourselves again."

"I hate them. I can't wait till tomorrow," Charles said vehemently,

Satisfied that he had fired up his cousin as much as was possible, Lucas now said to Lewis and Charles, "We don't make a move till Sam and Lukey take out the two sentries."

They perked up when they heard turkeys gobbling. They knew that the gobbles were fake sounds being made by Sam and Lukey, who were in place now, at the two sides of the building. They had sneaked up by skirting the woods around back.

Rufus said, "That's them. Get ready."

They tensed up and gripped their weapons tightly.

Once again Lewis leaned toward Jolene and whispered gruffly. "You mind now, girl, if you wanna stay alive."

Lukey and Sam suddenly appeared right behind the two sentries at opposite ends of the broad front porch— and they slit the soldiers' throats before they could cry out. They dropped their rifles with a clatter as their blood gushed out and they fell dead.

Rufus, Charles and Lewis ran up the steps onto the porch as Lukey and Sam wiped their bloody knives on the dead sentries' shirts, then pulled out their revolvers.

Then all five outlaws crashed through the doors of the trading post, their guns blazing.

BLAM! BLAM! BLAM! BLAM!

They gunned down three soldiers and a middle-aged woman with a bolt of yellow cloth in her hands.

A civilian in bibbed coveralls dove for a shotgun but

didn't manage to get it up and fire it before he died in a hail of bullets.

The outlaws' guns were hot and smoking and the place was filled with the acrid odor of burnt gunpowder.

Three civilians were in utter shock, backing away, futilely looking for a place to hide or some way to escape.

Rufus yelled, "The rest of you! Don't try to run or we'll blast you down!"

All three put their hands up. But Rufus laughed and blasted away at them. So did Sam, Charles and Lewis—and as they collapsed in pools of their own blood, Rufus said, "Fooled them! Gave them a moment of hope—but they shouldn't have believed me!"

Lukey tried to turn the handle of a closed door off to one side of the counter, but the door didn't budge, so he put his shoulder to it and splintered the jamb. When he burst in, he caught a trooper working a telegraph key and promptly shot him in the chest.

The trooper slumped down on the telegraph instrument and Lukey turned and yelled.

"Hey, Rufus, I just shot a guy that was gonna tell on us!"

"Tell on us how?"

"Tryin' to send a telegram—but I nailed him, the no-good bastard!"

14

Heck Thomas tied his horse to a hitching post in front of a low brown-stucco building with a sign above the door: UNITED STATES INDIAN POLICE, MUSKOGEE, OKLAHOMA. He stepped up to a front door with a placard on the glass: *Sam Sixkiller, Captain.*

Captain Sixkiller yelled, "Come on in, Heck!"

Heck entered, taking off his hat. He saw Sam Sixkiller sitting behind his desk, and another man standing to Sam's right.

Sam Sixkiller was a highly respected Cherokee policeman, but he dressed like a white man, in a three-piece brown suit with a gold watch chain on his vest. In his early forties, he had close-cropped brown hair and a neatly trimmed mustache.

Heck glanced at the other gentleman, whom he did not know, and said to Sixkiller, "How'd you know it was me before I even knocked, Sam?"

"Because I figured you'd show up here. This man is Corporal Paden Tolbert, one of my best men, always keeps tabs on things. He was nosing around, and a bartender told him you were in Muskogee yesterday, asking questions about Rufus Buck."

Paden Tolbert was Cherokee, like Sam Sixkiller, but he had straight black shoulder-length hair, and he was wearing the military-style blue uniform of the Indian Police, with a tin badge, short-brimmed round-topped hat and two yellow stripes on the sleeves of his tunic.

Heck said, "Glad to meet you, Corporal Tolbert."

"Call me Paden. From what I hear, nobody told you much. None of 'em ever wanna talk to strangers. Especially lawmen."

"You got that right," Heck said. "I thought I might have better luck if I came here."

Sam Sixkiller said, "I've arrested Rufus and his pals a couple times for petty theft or drunk and disorderly. I let them stew in a cell till they got their heads on sort of straight, then turned them loose. As far as I know, they never did anything worse, though."

Heck said, "I guess they was gonna go real bad sooner or later, Sam, you just didn't know it. Now they're in deep shit. They killed John Garrett just for a warm-up, then they raped two women that I know of and killed at least three men, one of them by lynching."

Obviously taken aback, Sam straightened up in his desk chair, looking glum and angry. Then he said, "I expect you want me to get up a posse to hunt them down."

"No, not yet," Heck said. "A posse bargin' around would just make 'em scramble. I'd like to zero in on wherever they might be holed up, then set up an ambush."

Paden Tolbert jumped in angrily. "And I suppose

you'd just shoot them down like dogs, just 'cause they're Indians?"

Heck blinked at the accusation, then narrowed his eyes and spoke soberly. "I'd get 'em pinned down, if I could. Then I'd call out for them to surrender. And if they didn't, well, no skin off of *my* nose."

Sam thought about this long and hard, then spoke in a levelheaded way. "Heck, don't get me wrong, but I'd like for you and Paden to team up on this manhunt. That way you can vouch for each other no matter how this ends. I don't want a Cherokee uprising if people think those boys got a vigilante kind of justice instead of a legal arrest and a fair trial."

Heck said, "I understand what you're sayin', Sam. But we've already got us an uprising on our hands. Or at the least, a vicious rampage."

————

HECK AND PADEN went to a saloon to get better acquainted and have some lunch. They ordered beers and hot roast beef sandwiches, plus shots of bourbon, and while they waited for their food to appear, they puffed on fat cigars and blew out clouds of smoke.

Paden leaned forward and asked Heck, "How long have you known Sam Sixkiller?"

Heck tapped cigar ashes onto the floor and sipped his beer before answering. "For a long time, I never knew Sam personally, but I heard of him. Then two years ago we collaborated on the hunt for the Dalton gang. But they got away from us by train, and hightailed it to California. Bob Dalton was the best I ever seen with a Colt revolver. He used to be a deputy marshal just like me at Fort

Smith, but he had a taste for bigger money, so he started stealing horses at first, then robbin' banks and trains. I was almost a little sad when him and his brothers got killed in Coffeeville, Kansas, 'bout three years ago."

They lapsed into silence for a moment, then clinked their shot glasses and tossed down the bourbon.

Paden said, "Sam Sixkiller's part white. His daddy was a Cherokee named Red Bird Sixkiller. He got in a gunfight with a bunch of Creeks and killed six of 'em, but his gun musta run outta bullets and he went down before he could reload. Little Sam's momma couldn't handle him after his pa was killed, so she let him be taken away to the Indian school in Pennsylvania, and that's how he got educated."

Heck said, "I know he fought for the Confederacy, which gives us somethin' in common, 'cause I did, too. How the hell did he end up in Muskogee—the most murderous town west of the Mississippi?"

"C'mon, it ain't that bad, Heck."

"Well, he's got forty men under his command, so maybe that makes him feel safe. But it shouldn't. It just takes one asshole to sneak up and plug him while he ain't lookin'."

Just then Sam Sixkiller barged through the swinging doors of the saloon, and a bunch of bar patrons stared at him as he strode to the far corner of the place where Heck and Paden were.

His breath exploding out of him, he said, "A telegraph operator from Western Union barged into my office a few minutes ago. He saw his keys starting to work, like someone was trying to send a message, but then it quit. He figured out that someone at the Army Trading Post was trying to make contact, but when he tried to respond, nothing happened, the line was dead. He thinks the wires must have been cut."

Heck pushed away from the table so hard that his chair fell over with a thud.

He said, "Oh, shit! Let's go!"

15

The same horses and wagons were still out in front of the Army Trading Post, but now the horses belonging to the Rufus Buck gang were hitched there, too. Gone was the travois that had held Jolene Palmer as a captive, all tied up.

At a table inside the place, Rufus, Sam, Lukey and Lewis were playing poker. Piles of poker chips and several stolen bottles of whisky were in front of them.

Charles Buck was not playing poker but was standing at a counter, slugging down whisky from a bottle he had commandeered for himself now that there was nobody alive who would object. He was in his glory, reaping the benefits of his new life outside the law, and he couldn't suppress a gleeful pride that his cousin Rufus had recruited him. And he had gladly taken part in the raid that they had successfully pulled off. He didn't see how they'd ever get caught, so long as they kept making sure not to leave any witnesses.

The bodies of four of their victims here at the trading station were still strung up from the rafters, like a badge of the gang's boldness and audacity. They had used the dead bodies for target practice with guns and knives. They were riddled with bullet holes, stab wounds and slice marks, and a half dozen of the knives sold at the trading post were still stuck in their torsos. There were puddles of blood beneath them on the floor and boot tracks through some of the puddles.

Jolene was still roped to the travois that used to be lashed Indian-fashion behind one of the horses. First they had loosened her bonds enough to allow her to let down her pants enough to pee, while they watched her do it and made lewd remarks. Then they tied her up again and carried the travois in here and stood it up in a corner with her still bound to it. She was all cramped up and squirming with stiffness and pain, and there was no position that she could get into to make the pain stop.

She was trying not to cry. She felt that she had to keep her wits about her in case she should somehow get a chance to escape. It was a wistful chance that seemed as distant as the man in the moon, but she forced herself not to give up hope. Her dad always got a kick out of her spunkiness and complimented her over and over, especially that time she broke and rode her own pony when she was only twelve. With a fresh shiver of sadness, it struck her that her twelfth birthday was only two years ago, and now that time of fresh hope and happiness seemed lost forever.

Charles went over to one of the dangling corpses and gave it a shove, then laughed as it swung to and fro, all the while looking straight into Jolene's eyes as if he had surely impressed her with his callousness. But it was an utterly grisly sight that made Jolene shudder and shut her eyes tight. Then, within seconds, she heard Charles's footsteps and fearfully opened her eyes again as he came near.

He said to her, "My, but you're a fine-looking piece of young stuff! Too bad I couldn't have met you at a church social. We coulda become boyfriend and girlfriend."

"When hell freezes over," she managed to say in a querulous voice.

"Why?" he said. "You don't like boys with pimples?"

He did have a bad case of acne. Pimples and blackheads all over his yellowish-brown face. By now Jolene knew that Charles was Rufus's cousin, but Rufus was dark brown, and Rufus had black eyes that glowed with some kind of brazen zeal that Charles lacked.

"I'm only seventeen," Charles said, "and I ain't afraid of nobody. And by the time I'm nineteen my pimples will be gone."

"You won't live that long," Jolene told him with sincerity. "You're gonna be shot or hanged."

"Like your daddy!" Charles snapped at her.

And she failed this time in her effort to appear unperturbed. Hot tears coursed down her cheeks.

He watched her cry, smiling at her. Then he tugged a filthy blue bandana from his hip pocket and blotted her tears, taking his time, doing it in a false show of tenderness.

He thought of backhanding her in her snotty face after he got done wiping it. In his opinion, women and girls were drawn to bad guys because they viewed them as strong and ruthless protectors. The bad boys—and Charles now looked upon himself as one of them—knew how to keep their women in line by beating them when they needed it, or even when they didn't. Sometimes their women secretly wanted it.

He put his face close to Jolene's and said, "What do you say to a woman with two black eyes?"

She wondered if he was going to hit her.

"Nothing," he said with a smirk. "She's already been told twice."

He laughed at his own bad joke. Then he reached out and cupped her face.

"C'mon, baby, be nice to me," he said. And he put his hands around her throat.

She wanted to spit on him, but she was scared he'd strangle her.

"Charles! Let her go!" Rufus called out. "Gotta deliver her in one piece."

She perked up, wondering where and to whom she was to be delivered. But she figured that it wasn't going to be good.

Rebuked, Charles shuffled over to the poker table and watched a hand being played. He stood a few feet back, for fear that the players might suspect him of looking over their shoulders and flashing a signal to one of the players about what was in the other players' hands. That kind of suspicion could get him shot in spite of the fact that he was Rufus's cousin.

Lukey said, "I call."

Sam said, "Me, too."

They each pushed a stack of chips into the pot.

Lewis threw his cards down so hard that his knuckles slammed the table. "*Ow!*" he said, and licked a couple of his fingers.

Lukey and Sam laughed at him.

Rufus said, "Too heavy for me. I'm out."

Lukey laid three cards down face up and said, "Three sixes."

Sam said, "Shit! I thought I had a winner! I only got three *deuces!*"

"Too bad," said Lukey, and he scooped up the pot.

"Deal, Mister Winner," Sam said irritably.

Lukey started gathering the deck together, so he could re-shuffle.

Charles wandered back over to the corner where Jolene was tied to the travois. Slyly, he lowered his voice and whispered to her, "Hey, babe. I like you. Want me to help you?"

"Help me do what?" she said tremulously, suppressing a kernel of hope.

"If you promise to be nice to me, I could loosen your ropes," he said. "The rest would be up to you. Or else I could run away with you and help you dodge them. You'd have a better chance that way."

She was desperate enough to take him up on his offer. But just as she was thinking about it and hoping that it might be real, he burst into coarse laughter, spewing spittle into her face.

She started to cry and Charles kept on laughing.

Still chortling, he ambled back over to the poker table.

"What were you sayin' to her?" Rufus asked gruffly.

"Just fuckin' with her," Charles said.

"We hafta clear outta here," Rufus said sharply.

"What's the hurry?" Sam said. "I'm havin' fun."

Rufus said, "That guy Lukey shot tryin' to use the telegraph. What if he got through to somebody?"

"Yeah," Lukey agreed. "Like Judge Parker's office or the soldiers at Fort Smith."

Lewis pooh-poohed their worries. "They couldn't get here in less than three hours at a fast gallop."

"And they'd have to get themselves together first," Sam added.

Rufus gave in a little, saying, "So shut up, drink up and deal another hand."

Charles said, "What about Jolene? Don't we have to pretty her up?"

Lukey snickered lecherously. "We get her lookin' much prettier, I'm gonna have a hard time controllin' myself. I'm already havin' a *hard* time, know what I mean? Why can't I have my way with her, Rufus? Just once or twice—what's the difference?"

Rufus said, "Because then she'll be damaged goods and we'll have to sell her too cheap. Peta Nocona has been known to skin people alive. I'm not bullshitting. His favorite thing is young, white virgins."

Lukey said, "Well, that's *my* thing, too, Rufus!" And he let loose a belly laugh.

Sam said, "Me, too!"

They all laughed uproariously.

Rufus said, "Hey, Lewis, you been lookin' glum and sloppin' down a whole lot of whisky, more than you used to. Don't you *like* bein' with us?"

"I feel bad about that one old lady with the blue cloth in her hands. She looked a lot like one of my favorite aunts, except she was white."

Lukey sneered at Lewis for his weakness and said, "When it comes to whites, ain't none of 'em innocent. They took our land, didn't they? They killed us off by the thousands."

Rufus said, "Our ancestors lived in places called Michigan, Louisiana and Florida. But the white people wanted our land, so their armies made all of them walk over a thousand miles, to where we live now. Thousands of them got sick and died."

"My grandfather told me about it," Lukey said. "They called it the Trail of Tears. The whites called it the Indian Removal Act."

Rufus said, "It was all about grabbing our land because we were weak and didn't have good weapons. The Great Spirit made that land for us. The Indians scoffed at the idea that anybody could own the earth. But the whites took it and fenced it in with barbed wire."

Lewis nodded somberly and said, "But they're still too powerful, Rufus. We'll have our way for a little while, but they'll hunt us down and kill us."

"Not if we scare them badly enough," Rufus said, with an effort at believing his own words. "If we rape and butcher enough of them, they'll pack up and go back where they came from and give us back our land. At least that is what I hope."

16

The main street of Fort Smith was quiet in the intense heat of an August afternoon as Tommy Palmer shuffled along with his head down, feeling like the most lonely boy in the world. He couldn't shake the hideous memories of all that had been done to him and his family. He was drawn to the apothecary and he wondered if what he had seen in the big window the other day would still be there. He hoped it would be.

Once again he took in the grisly sight of Maoma July in death with that pitchfork resting against him, and the display fueled a reservoir of hatred that momentarily overtook his grief. He wished he had seen the pitchfork sticking out of Maoma, but Heck Thomas had pulled it out without allowing Tommy to go down to the barn. Then, after digging the graves for Tommy's family members, Heck and George had put Maoma's body in the bed of the buckboard to take it to Fort Smith to claim the reward. It was $2,000 and the two lawmen said the money would go to Tommy and his grandparents because

Jolene had probably been the one who killed Maoma, and Tommy fervently hoped that his sister had done it. But that thought was also met with a tremor of fear. Because if Jolene had killed the outlaw, of course the rest of the gang would know it, and that'd make them want to do worse to Jolene than they had done to the rest of Tommy's family.

He shuddered every time images of the carnage he had seen came unbidden into his mind. They haunted his dreams, but also his daytime hours. He had gotten enough of a glimpse of what had been done to his mother to realize, in the deepest part of his young soul, that the men who had committed those foul acts were irredeemably evil and even more vicious than they had shown themselves to be when they had killed his father. The depraved ugliness, the bloody desecration of human flesh wrought by them at the ranch, had plummeted Tommy's recognition of evil to a new and more profound depth in his tormented psyche.

He jumped and let out a shriek when someone came up on him from behind, giving him a wavering glimpse of a ghostlike figure in the mortuary window. He trembled, scared to turn around and look—and when he finally risked it, it was the hangman, George Maledon, that he found himself looking at.

"Easy, son," George said, placing a hand on Tommy's shoulder.

Tommy was still shaken enough that he couldn't speak.

Maledon said soothingly, "He can't hurt you anymore, Tommy. That's what I tell myself each time I pull the lever on 'em. I fix it so they can't hurt anyone ever again. Maybe I'm crazy, but I confess that the clunk of the rope when it straightens out is a very satisfying thing to me."

In his shaky, boyish voice, Tommy said, "What about the ones that are still on the loose? I have nightmares about them. My grandma comes in and hugs me till I quit crying. The two boys that live downstairs heard me one night, and now they never miss a chance to make fun of me."

Maledon was at a loss at first. He didn't think he had done a good job of raising his own daughter, or else she wouldn't have hooked up with the wrong man, and she'd probably still be alive. But he felt sorry for Tommy after all the boy had gone through, and he wanted to help, even though he doubted his ability to do so in any meaningful way.

In his desperation to come up with something, a thought struck him and he said, "Those boys you're talkin' about don't realize how brave you are, but I do 'cause I seen it firsthand. Do you want to make them open their dumb eyes about you? I know a newspaper reporter who'd want to talk to you and publish your story."

Tommy never thought he'd ever do anything that would get him into a newspaper, and he wasn't sure it was anything he wanted. He considered it, and slowly shook his head no. "I don't want that gang to read about me...Rufus Buck and his gang that killed my dad. They killed my whole family. They might come after me and my grandma and grandpap."

Maledon said, "I don't blame you for bein' scared, Tommy. But you'll prob'ly never see them again. The gang, I mean. They'll run and hide, like the rats they are. But Heck Thomas'll catch up with them and bring 'em in dead or alive. And my ropes will be waitin' for any of 'em he fails to gun down."

But Tommy hung his head and said, "I don't think my

nightmares are gonna go away, Mr. Maledon. I'm scared about my sister, too. My grandma keeps praying for her all day long, and I don't know if it does any good. Where do you think Jolene is? Do you think she's still alive?"

"I hope so, son. I truly hope so."

17

Heck Thomas and Paden Tolbert didn't waste any time getting to the U.S. Army Trading Post, but they didn't run their horses to death either. It took them about four hours to get to within a few hundred yards of their objective, and they were hot, thirsty and tired, but they stopped right there because they didn't want to chance getting picked off. Figuring that Rufus Buck could've been smart enough to post a lookout or two, Heck said, "We know they're reckless and stupid, but we can't let our guard down. We gotta operate as if they've got some smarts."

With this in mind, they didn't charge right up to the place; instead they circled around and emerged from the surrounding woods. Several horses, one of them harnessed to a wagon, were tethered to the hitching posts.

"Too damn quiet," Paden whispered.

Nodding in agreement, Heck said, "We're gonna find dead people inside. The wagon and horses must've belonged to the victims."

"Let's go in," Paden whispered. "Could be wounded in there still alive."

With their rifles at the ready, but keeping their pistols holstered for the time being, they crept forward and took shelter behind a hitching post and a wagon.

Heck glanced at Paden to make sure he was all set, then yelled, "You in there! We're U.S. marshals! Drop your weapons and come on out!"

They got no response. Not a word, not a sound.

Paden shouted, "Show us empty hands, boys! You make a wrong move, you're dead!"

Again they got no response.

Heck motioned Paden to stay back, and Paden covered Heck with his rifle as Heck started forward in a crouch.

When Heck got up onto the porch, he saw the two sentries lying apart from each other with their throats slit. But he didn't linger on that dreadful sight. He tried the knob on the door and flashed a surprised look back at Paden when the door easily swung open. He eased past the jamb and peered inside. Then, with a look of dismay, he backpedaled and motioned for Paden to join him.

They both entered the trading station, and were shaken by the sight of so many dead bodies, including four that were hanging from the rafters.

Trying not to step in the puddles of blood seeping into the plank floor, they worked their way through the place, peering into the distorted faces of each and every corpse, in case they might find among them a friend or an acquaintance. It was a task familiar to both of them, yet they never got used to it. For Heck, the sight of men dead from bullet wounds or torn apart by cannon shot went back to his time as a boy in the civil war. And for the much younger man, Paden Tolbert, in a fifty-mile radius of Muskogee, his home office, there were more murders than in any other place west of the Mississippi.

They worked their way among shelves of canned goods, dry goods and so forth, keeping their guns drawn for fear of encountering any gang members who might have been left there, perhaps wounded but still alive. It was unlikely prospect, and luckily it did not happen. But the two lawmen were not about to take chances.

Heck opened the door to the little office where the telegraph setup was, and stepped around a dead soldier with bullet holes in him, his face frozen in a look of surprise as if he did not expect to die today. Heck saw what was left of the equipment the man had been trying to use in his final moments, parts of it scattered on the desk and on the floor.

When he came back out, he told Paden, "They didn't climb the pole to cut the telegraph line, they just ripped the wires loose and smashed the machine. But we've gotta get in touch with Sam Sixkiller and tell him to get some men out here."

Paden said, "Maybe we can find a farmer or a rancher who can hand-carry a message to Sam in Muskogee. He'll need to post some guards for this place so it won't be further ransacked. And a grave detail from Fort Smith. With some of the bodies being civilian and some military, it's gonna be hell identifying them and notifying the next of kin."

"Well, it's not a job for you and me," Heck said. "We'll have to secure this place as best we can, but we can't break off our pursuit, or there's gonna be more victims. We're gonna need to figure out where this gang of savages might be headed."

Paden shot Heck a raised-eyebrow look, and Heck

said, "Come off it, Paden. I know *all* Injuns ain't savages, but these ones *are.*"

"Okay, okay, no offense taken," Paden said. "They're savages all right. Question is, how did they get that way? And I admit I can't fathom it."

"Ours is not to reason why," Heck said. "Our job is to put an end to it."

Paden said, "I was glad none of my soldier friends was killed in there. I thought I might've slightly known one of those poor fellows that was hangin' from the rafters, but his face was so swollen purple that I couldn't be sure."

"You have to push it out of your mind, that's all there is to it," Heck said.

"I know that as well as you do," said Paden. "It looks like rain is comin' in. We better get our butts outside and start looking for tracks before they get washed away."

They went back out onto the dirt road and looked closely at the churned-up dirt.

Paden said, "It looks like the killers headed westerly."

"One of their horses is pulling something," Heck conjectured. "Maybe a travois. Look at that track. No wheel marks, just drag marks."

"Makes sense, in a way. Indians might use a travois to carry loot in a rolled-up blanket or a big leather sack."

"Or a girl captive," Heck speculated. "They might tie her up that way to take her with them wherever they're going. Jolene is only fourteen. I only know what she looks like from Tommy's description, but I didn't see anybody that young among the dead."

Paden said, "Could be they're keeping her alive. Maybe for ransom."

"I wouldn't put anything past the crazy bastards," Heck said. "But why would they think anybody would pay big money for Jolene? Her family was far from wealthy, by the looks of their ranch."

"Speakin' of that, who's runnin' it now?" Paden asked.

"Grandparents on the father's side have it up for sale. Meantime, they hurried up and sold off the little herd of livestock so it wouldn't get rustled. It didn't fetch much money, but what there was, they put aside for Tommy—and Jolene, if we ever find her."

"Well, there you go," Paden said. "That'd provide plenty enough ransom money for a poor Indian who never had a pot to piss in. More money than Rufus Buck ever seen in one place. But who knows how these assholes think."

"All they're thinkin' about is rapin' and killin'," Heck said. "And we gotta put a stop to it."

18

M uskogee was crowded with trail hands, drifters, farmer and ranchers, some with their families. Mothers with children in hand trekked in and out of the various stores on Main Street. It was a big day for horse racing, one of the most exciting things that ever happened around here. The track on the outskirts of town was two miles long, and lots of people hurried back and forth between the shops and the races, and they carried baskets of food, jars of lemonade and bottles of whisky. Spectators lined both sides of the race track and scrambled to bet on long-legged geldings, some of them with U.S. Army brands on their rumps.

The horses and riders lined up for a dropped-flag start. And when the flag was dropped, shouts and cheers from the onlookers nearly drowned out the immediate sound of pounding hooves.

Sam Sixkiller and his wife, Fannie, had come to town today, but they weren't interested in horse racing. They had to pick up Sam's medicine from a drugstore, and they wished they didn't have to fight the crowds and the noise, but Sam wasn't feeling well and needed the prescription. He was driving their horse-drawn buggy when they pulled up in front of the drugstore. He was dressed as usual in a three-piece brown suit. Fannie was a comely woman in a ruffled dress she had bought from the Sears Roebuck catalogue.

Sam said, "I'll keep the reins handy if you'll go in and get it."

She said, "Do you really think it's doing you any good, Sam? I read about it. It's mostly alcohol and paregoric."

"Well, it seems to help me sleep."

She sighed as she stepped down from the buggy, gave him an impatient look, then went into the drugstore. At first she saw nobody behind the counter. She peered between shelves stocked with dozens of herbs and nostrums, and no one was there stocking the shelves.

She called out, "Hellooo? Mr. Foster?"

Foster came out from a back room. He said, "Sorry, Fannie. Nature called. I have Sam's medicine right here. Seventy-five cents, as usual."

She took some coins out of a dainty little purse, handed them to Mr. Foster, and he held up a little bottle of paregoric, then plunked it into a bag and handed it to her.

In a hurry to go and get away from the racetrack crowd, she said, "Good day, Mr. Foster. Sam's out there waiting."

Mr. Foster said, "See you next time, Fannie. Tell Sam I hope his bowels settle down. He's under a powerful lot of stress."

"You can say that again. I wish he were in a different line of work."

She went out into the street and stopped when she

saw her husband dozing in the carriage, his head nodding onto his chest.

"Sam, wake up," she told him. "If you're gonna nap, wait till we get home."

She reached out and touched his shoulder—and he sagged and fell sideways onto the wagon seat.

She froze and her mouth gaped open in shock.

His throat had been slit from ear to ear, and he was wearing a grisly bib of blood.

She screamed.

And just then a horse came galloping from around the side of the drugstore—and Rufus Buck was in the saddle.

Riding as fast as his horse could go, he gunned Fannie down with three rapid-fire bullets, and she fell into the dirt street, pumping a geyser of blood from a severed artery.

Rufus looked back over his shoulder and saw Mr. Foster standing in the doorway of the drugstore looking straight at him. He spurred his horse—the one stolen from Chuck Palmer—and galloped at breakneck speed down the dusty street and out of sight.

The throng of people walking toward the racetrack whooped and cheered and stared after him as if he were a victorious rider crossing the finish line.

19

Jolene stared through the wooden bars inches away from her face. She was in a cage made of rude wooden poles lashed together with rawhide. It was in the bed of a wagon with side rails, and Lewis Davis, Lukey Davis and Sam Sampson used additional lengths of rawhide to tie the cage to the rails. Then they unfolded and stretched out a leather tarp and whipped it over the cage and tied it down, blanketing Jolene in darkness. She was cramped and scared and at the same time she was relieved—because for now they wouldn't be able to touch her.

All night long she had been kept tied up and gagged, on a dirt floor in an old bunkhouse full of mice and spider webs. She could hear noises outside that made her surmise that a cage was being built for her because earlier she had overheard Rufus telling them to do it. Then they had come for her and dragged her out into the sunshine, and had giggled while they all ran their hands over every part of her body, making all kinds of lewd comments, asking her if she was enjoying it and saying she must be "getting all hot and bothered."

At least in the dark cage she was safe from their taunts and their sadistic caresses—for the time being. She had no idea what was in store for her, except what she had overheard the other day, that apparently they were intending to sell her to somebody. Some pervert, in other words. She was filed with dread at the very thought.

Suddenly she heard galloping hooves—but she couldn't see what was happening. She recoiled against the wooden bars, an automatic reflex, as if they could offer protection instead of helpless imprisonment. She knew it was Rufus Buck arriving in a hurry as soon as she heard him speak. She also knew he was probably still riding the horse that once belonged to her father, and for that she hated him even more.

RUFUS BUCK JUMPED down from the horse that he now called Blue Demon. He had ridden the animal to a lather in his escape from Muskogee. Holding the reins, he said, "I think there's gonna be a posse after us. I was spotted makin' a run for it."

"Posse will take a while," Lukey said, "How will they know where you went after you hightailed it outta town?"

"They might be able to track me. My horse tossed a shoe and I heard it clink against a rock. I'm surprised I heard it 'cause his hooves were poundin' so damn hard. Then he started limpin'."

"I told you a couple days ago that the heads were worn off of the nails," Lukey said.

"Well, I wasn't about to linger around a blacksmith shop long enough to get myself arrested. I'm gonna take your horse, Sam, so you'll be drivin' the wagon."

Getting more and more disgruntled, Lukey said, "So now we might have a posse catchin' up to us. Fuck this shit!"

Rufus took John Garrett's badge out of his pocket and pinned it on his coat. "If anybody asks any nosy questions, I'm Sheriff Garrett, like before, and you guys're my posse. I'm glad I at least killed Sam Sixkiller—and nailed his wife, too. I been wantin' to get him for a long time. He was a disgrace—a Cherokee who captured other Cherokees and put 'em in jail."

Sam piped up, asking, "How far away is the guy who's gonna buy Jolene?"

"His name is Peta Nocona," Rufus said. "I'm sure you've heard of him even if you've never seen him. He keeps a low profile most of the time so the law doesn't latch onto him. He lives in a house near the Creek Nation, about twenty miles from here. We should be there by dusk. He's already got three wives, if not more. But he doesn't like 'em once they get outta their teens. Sometimes he drowns 'em, and sometimes he keeps 'em around to wash clothes and chew leather."

"Ha!' Sam barked. "That's what women are good for —screwin' 'em and makin' 'em work."

Rufus nodded in agreement. He said, "The whites treat their women like they're so sweet and dainty their shit don't stink. Indians know that a good wife needs to be beaten so she'll stay in her place."

20

Wearing knickers, suspenders and a slouch hat—
stuff he'd never have been caught wearing at
the ranch, or even on visits to Fort Smith with his father
—Tommy Palmer knocked on George Maledon's cabin
door. He could smell rain in the air, but it hadn't poured
down yet, and he hoped that it wouldn't. He already felt
sissified in the clothes his grandma made him wear
today, and on top of it he didn't want to look like a
soaked rat. It was true that some of the town boys
dressed this way on Sundays, but usually only the richest
and snobbiest. But Grandma said he had to look his best
for the reporter he was supposed to meet this afternoon,
after church. He had felt conspicuously odd-looking all
through the sermon, and had kept his head down, buried
in his hymn book. As owners of a drug store, his grandparents were considered "gentry" in this town of eleven-
thousand "ordinary folks," and he almost wished that
they weren't. Some of the other kids in the pews were
smirking at him and he knew they would've snickered if

they weren't in church. One good thing was that they had ridden there in a carriage that was parked close by when church let out, so he was able to jump in right away, avoiding some of the kids who were the snottiest.

Mr. Maledon smiled at him when he opened the cabin door, and said, "Well, hello, Tommy! I wasn't sure you'd show up."

"Don't laugh at me," he blurted. "My grandma made me wear this stuff."

"Nothin' wrong with gettin' spiffed up once in a while. I've been known to do it myself."

He winked, and Tommy wondered if he was referring to the black suit and black tie he always wore when was going to hang somebody. Tommy had never seen one of the hangings but he had heard all about them.

"I was scared to come here," he admitted.

"You don't need to be," George said, still smiling. "I'm not even wearing my guns."

"Not of you," Tommy said.

"I know, I'm just joking with you. Come on in."

Tommy entered timidly and for the first time saw Seth Crosby, who was sitting on the edge of George's bunk. Unlike George, who was thin but wiry, a "man's man" as Tommy's dad might have put it, Crosby looked meek and timid. And the brown suit he was wearing looked a bit worse for the wear.

George sat at his desk, and Tommy couldn't help staring at the ropes, nooses, chains and shackles hanging from pegs above him, on the log wall.

The reporter arose and reached out his hand. "My name's Seth Crosby, Tommy. I write for *Frank Leslie's Illustrated Newspaper*. I also write dime novels, and I'm working on one about Mr. Maledon."

Shaking Crosby's hand, which felt pudgy and soft, Tommy said, "I know. George told me."

Crosby cleared his throat and said, "Mr. Maledon also told me what you went through, Tommy. It seems you're a pretty brave little boy."

"I don't feel brave, I feel scared. All the time. Even in my dreams."

"Do you talk about that with your grandmother? Or your preacher?"

"No, not much. The other boys here in town want to hear all about it, though. And when I don't want to talk about it, they get mad and poke fun at me. They even put their hands around their necks and make choking sounds."

Tommy had to hold back tears when he said that, and he tried to force back the images of his father's death that ran through his mind.

Crosby said, "Well, I won't poke fun of you, and neither will Mr. Maledon."

"I know George won't. He's been my friend."

"I want to be your friend, too. I think it's important for people to know your story. And I think it will be helpful for you to just open up about it. It's a form of therapy. There's a man named Dr. Sigmund Freud who has explored those kinds of possibilities. Do you understand?"

"Yes, sir. But I want to kill the people that killed my family and took my sister."

Crosby was taken aback by Tommy's youthful vehemence. But he said, "It's normal to want revenge. But sometimes it can do more damage to the one who exacts it that the ones who are on the receiving end."

Digesting this, Tommy was not convinced right away.

He said, "My grandma cries every night. She muffles it with her pillow, but I still hear her."

The reporter didn't know what to say.

George Maledon got up from his desk chair and put his hand on Tommy's shoulder.

Tommy looked up at him, and his tears began to fall.

21

On their way to Peta Nocona's place, the Rufus Buck gang approached a farm house that Lukey had previously scouted. The rain that they had anticipated had come down like a deluge, but when it was over, the sky cleared miraculously and became crystal blue, and the land dried up quickly in the burning sunshine, as if had never been wet.

Rufus Buck led the gang toward the front of the farmhouse and put his right hand up, signaling a halt. The others pulled up around him. Sam Sampson couldn't get in too close with the others, since he was driving the wagon with the tarp lashed down over Jolene's cage.

"Wait here," Rufus said. "I'll go up on the porch."

The house was rudely built like most others around here, probably built with neighbors coming long distances to pitch in. The walls were planks painted red with white trim, and it had a tin roof and a big railed-in porch.

Lukey said, "I smell fried chicken."

Rufus rapped on the door and a big-bellied man in

rumpled trousers and wide brown suspenders opened the door. He didn't make clomping sounds on the floor as he emerged, because he wasn't wearing any boots, just dirty white socks. He looked to be about fifty years old or so, and had gone bald on top, but sported a thick gray beard.

He eyed Rufus warily, and became even more nervous when he saw the other four ruffians hanging back, at the edge of the dirt road.

Rufus said, "We're on our way to the Creek Nation, and we been travelin' for a day and a half. We was thinkin' kinda hopefully that maybe your missus would cook us a meal if we paid her twenty dollars."

"How'd you know I have a missus?" the man asked, as if he was thinking they might have scouted the place.

"Just figured it. A man don't like to live alone out here."

"What's your name?" Spencer asked sharply.

"Sheriff John Garrett, Indian Police." Rufus fingered the badge. "We're tryin' to hunt down a bad man named Rufus Buck. You ever hear of him?"

"Yeah, we did, just yesterday at the general store. Seems like nobody's seen him around here, though."

"Well, he musta passed through without causin' a ruckus," Rufus said. "He's been runnin' from us and we intend to catch up with him and bring him to justice. We think he's aimin' to hide out among the Creeks. But we need provisions if we're gonna stay on his trail. We're about half starved and worn out. You got any grub for us?"

The man looked so nervous that Rufus didn't think he was buying in to the story. But what could he do about it? The odds were five to one. He was totally right to sense danger, but he was trapped and outnumbered.

"Well, let me ask my wife," Spencer said, obviously hoping nothing bad would happen. "She's fryin' some chicken, and there might be enough."

He went back into the house, and Rufus turned around and gave his gang a thumbs-up.

Lukey sidled over to the back of the wagon, lifted a corner of the tarp, and gave Jolene a gruff warning. "We're gonna be here a while, girl. You better not make a fuss, or we'll kill *you and* these damn farmers."

The man of the house came to the door again and motioned Rufus and the boys to come on in. Standing by the potbellied stove in the sparely furnished front room, he said, "I'm Spencer Patterson." He forced a smile. "Mind if I ask for the twenty dollars in advance? Ellie says she's got more chicken parts, and she'll put 'em in the skillet. You'll get 'em with green beans and mashed potatoes."

Rufus handed over a twenty-dollar bill, and Spencer pocketed it. Then, with a failed attempt at a smile, he said, "Come on into the kitchen and spread out around the table. You're gonna leave here with your bellies full."

"Oh, no question we'll be happy when we leave," Rufus said. "You've already made us feel like we belong."

Lukey and Sam snickered, but the other two managed to restrain themselves.

An ominous feeling of despair descended upon Spencer Patterson.

22

Heck Thomas and Paden Tolbert tracked the horse with the missing shoe for thirteen miles heading out of Muskogee in the direction that the escaping murderer of Sam Sixkiller and his wife had reportedly gone. No doubt from the description that it was Rufus Buck operating all by his lonesome without the other gang members. The two lawmen decided that he probably relished the role of a lone assassin and figured that he'd have the best chance of pulling it off that way. By the same token, Heck and Paden figured they'd have the best chance of catching up to the gang if they did it as a duo instead of with a posse full of clattering hooves stirring up clouds of dust wherever it went. Besides, Sam had been their good friend and esteemed colleague and they wanted to be the ones to capture and kill the gang or see them hanged.

Going at it with the necessary patience, they had already been into their hunt for over three hours before the rain came. They took shelter under some over-hanging rocks, which didn't totally protect them from windblown water, and smoked hand-rolled cigarettes. They knew the heavy rain would wipe out all the hoof marks they had been following, and they'd have to somehow get lucky and latch onto some other sign.

Paden became more chatty than usual as they stood under the rocks and smoked while they got doused with rain. He brought up the time about ten years ago when Sam took down Dick Glass, the notorious leader of a gang of horse rustlers and bootleggers. Glass's method was to sell his stolen horses and use the money to buy illegal whisky in Texas, which he'd bring back across the Red River and sell it at a huge profit. "Sam put an end to that," Paden said with a gleeful chuckle. "Him and another marshal by the name of Charles LeFlore ambushed Glass and his crew where they was hidin' out in the Chickasaw nation, and Sam plugged Glass before he could even draw his pistol."

"Yep," Heck acknowledged. "The rest of Glass's crew —about four of 'em—was done in, in the firefight. Two against five, but it didn't bother Sam or Charlie. I knew Charlie, too. I worked with him for a time and we made a pile of bounty money."

"I like bounties," Paden said. "Worth a lot more than a fixed salary."

"Shit, we couldn't live on just our wages," Heck said. "And Judge Parker knows it."

"He treats us good and the outlaws bad," said Paden.

"He treats 'em the way they need to be treated," Heck said perfunctorily.

Paden stepped out from under the rocks and peered into the sky for a long moment. "The rain's gone," he said. "So what's our next move?"

Heck said, "All I can think to do is keep headin' in the same direction, try to pick up where we left off. It was a quick rain. Hard but quick. It dried up for Rufus as well as us. And he's prob'ly still on that horse that tossed the shoe."

"I agree it's our best shot," Paden said.

"Our best and only shot," Heck affirmed.

They rode slowly for three miles or so, and then they spotted the same kind of marks that had been their guide before the rain. They patiently and doggedly followed them, and they led to an old bunkhouse.

They spent some time checking out the horseshoe tracks and wagon tracks in the dirt.

Paden said, "We missed 'em, Heck. Looks they was here, but now they're gone."

Heck said, "Either they put a new shoe on the horse we been tracking, or else none of them are on that same horse anymore."

They walked around the side of the bunkhouse and saw a horse tethered to a tree branch.

Heck picked up the right rear hoof and saw that it was without a shoe. Just pieces of nails sticking out. He showed Paden. Then he said, "Well, this is, or was, Rufus's mount. So he must have joined up with the others and now they're headed somewhere."

Paden said, "The wagon tracks might be easier to follow."

But Heck's thoughts were off on a different tack.

Paden looked at Heck and said, "What's noodlin' your noggin?"

Heck said, "I hate to think it, but I don't believe Jolene is still alive. Or else, why wouldn't they already be makin' a ransom demand?"

23

Jolene was sweating profusely and burning up with the heat inside the cage. When the rain was pounding down so hard, just a while ago, it sounded like a hundred drumsticks hitting the leather tarp all at once and not about to let up. She had wished that some of the drops would leak in so she could cup her hands and get a drink of rainwater and douse it on her face. At least it was cooler then, but now it was stifling hot again. It was like an oven red with coals for roasting a freshly butchered pig, which was a task she had hated back at the ranch, but now she wished fervently and despairingly that those days were back.

During her waking hours, she was horrified by the way she had killed the gang member called Maoma, who had chased her into the barn. She could almost feel the terror and the final thrusts. But in her nightmares *she* was the one being impaled on the bloody tines, instead of him, and she would wake up clawing at her chest, trying to pull the pitchfork out.

She had heard Rufus's cronies muttering about a farmhouse and a home-cooked meal. Dark mutterings. Because she could tell from the few words she could make out that they weren't going to be satisfied with just the food. She had horrible memories of what they had done to her mother and her grandparents, and she felt guilty that she had survived and they hadn't. But her survival didn't bode well. She had overheard their talk about selling her into a slavery of unwilling sex. They reminded Jolene of Satan licking his lips, which was what her preacher said Satan would do when he welcomed sinners into Hell.

She had to try to escape. Maybe she'd get a chance because the gang was so distracted by their gleeful anticipation of the atrocities that they intended to commit against the folks who lived here. She felt bad that their misfortune might work to her benefit, but on the other hand, if she could make a run for it, she might be able to get help.

The cage door was chained and locked. The only way to get out was to loosen some of the rawhide that held the wooden poles together. And even if she could manage that, next she'd have to undo the tarp that had been tossed over the cage and lashed down. It seemed hopeless. But she had to try. She managed to squeeze her fingers between two of the poles where their ends met and were held in place by coils of rawhide. But they were tied so tight that the knots wouldn't budge, and she clawed at them and broke two fingernails.

Hopelessness overwhelmed her and she had to stifle her sobs for fear that the murderers might hear her. She had been warned not to try to sound a warning. Maybe they wouldn't kill her, since they thought she was worth money. That only seemed logical. But on the other hand they were viciously cruel and ruthlessly impulsive, and they didn't always operate in the realm of logic.

24

Rufus and his cohorts were feeling well satisfied by
the home-cooked meal served to them by Ellie
Patterson, Spencer's wife. She was an attractive woman,
about thirty-five years old, in a plain homespun dress not
suitable for Sunday-come-to-meetin' but just fine for
around the house, and it had been washed so often that
it clung to her in an alluring way. The young murderers
eyed her lecherously, and quite openly, as she moved
among them picking up used dishes and utensils. They
didn't care if they offended her husband, who was still
sitting at the head of the table looking glum and scared.

Lukey said to Spencer's wife, in a pantomime of good
manners, "That was a mighty fine meal, Ellie. We're
much obliged. We need a lot of energy to go after the bad
guys."

"And Rufus Buck is one of the very worst," Rufus
said.

Sam Sampson and Charles Buck openly snickered,
and Spencer Patterson shot them an alarmed look.

Lukey said, "I'm curious about somethin', Spencer. How did you come to own this farm?"

"It was left to me by my daddy. And my momma. Me and Ellie built a cabin down the way, so we'd be close enough to help them work the fields, and we done just that till they got old and passed away. We have a helper who lives in the cabin now, and we moved in here."

"Sounds pretty sweet," Charles said, as if accusing them of something.

Ellie said, "Well, we get by. But it takes a whole lot of hard work."

Lukey persisted in his line of questioning. "Now, I can't help wonderin', how did your daddy and your momma come to own this farm, Spencer? Who did they pay for it?"

"There was nobody to pay for it," Spencer said self-defensively. "The government opened up Arizona Territory for settlement by folks who wanted to come here and make somethin' of themselves. It was an opportunity that didn't exist back east."

Rufus asked a more probing question. "It didn't bother you—or your daddy—that there were Indians livin' on this land?"

"Never thought about it," said Spencer, even more warily. "The government of the United States makes the law, not the Indians, and they didn't care to farm the land anyhow. It was goin' to waste."

Rufus and his boys chortled sarcastically at this.

Ellie once more came to her husband's defense. "We didn't do anything wrong, and neither did my husband's parents. Everything they did was perfectly legal."

"Well, by whose laws?" Rufus shot back at her. "Indians have laws. Maybe our laws was the ones that was broken just so the land this farm is on could be stolen."

Lukey raised his voice angrily. "The whole damn thing pisses me off. It shouldn't ought to be that way, Ruf—I mean...er...Sheriff."

It was clear that he almost spoke Rufus's real name on purpose. It was part of a cat-and- mouse game that he and Rufus were playing and getting a kick out of.

Sam took it upon himself to open the game up and let the Pattersons know in no uncertain terms that the strangers they had let into their home were a mean and dangerous threat. Harshly, he said, "Let's get on with our business here, Rufus."

Lewis backed him up, saying, "Yeah, we might not have much time."

Rufus spoke to Spencer and Ellie bluntly and commandingly. "All right, let's negotiate. We enjoyed the meal you made for us, but it's not all we want. Food is only one of our animal appetites. Let's just say...twenty dollars for the meal, which we already paid—and another twenty dollars for the...*appetites.*"

Spencer got the meaning and was totally appalled. "Are you *crazy?*" he barked. "My wife is not gonna let you violate her!"

Smirking, Rufus said, "Why? Don't you like the price? We can up it by fifty cents."

Lukey stood up, advanced upon the farm owners, put his Colt up against Spencer's head and said, "Here's your chance, Ellie. You wanna save your husband's life?"

Rufus said, "At least we're givin' you a choice. That's more than *our* ancestors got. Their land was stolen and their women and children were raped and killed."

Spencer said, "You're crazy out of your mind! We had nothin' to do with what happened all those years ago!"

"You keep callin' me *crazy*, but I'm the one who's in control here. Have you noticed that? Or are you too damn stupid?"

Touching her husband's shoulder, Ellie pleaded, "Spencer, please...I'll do whatever they say, if it'll save both our lives."

Rufus said, "That sounds sensible to me, Ellie. And if you gotta do it, you may as well have fun at it. You only get out of it what you put into it. Right, boys?"

They guffawed, and Lewis blurted, "Right on!"

Sam said, "I don't want no sloppy seconds, Rufus. I wanna be first."

Lewis said, "Me, too! Let's draw. High card wins."

He took a deck of bent and dirty poker cards out of his pocket and fanned them out. One by one, each of the other gang members drew a card. When Charles looked at him, he let out a whoop.

"*Woo-hoo!* I got an *ace!* Can any of you boys tie it?"

Sam said, "That ain't fair! You're just a kid!"

"You're only two years older'n me!" Charles shot back at him.

The rest of them looked at the cards they'd drawn.

Rufus said, "I drew a king. I'm second."

Spencer and Ellie were cowering in each other's arms, but none of the gang paid any attention to them.

Sam griped, "I drew a lowly six."

Lukey said, "So what. I'm gonna be low man on the totem pole. I got a damn three!"

"I'm ahead of you at least," Lewis chimed in, showing a five of clubs.

Rufus said, "Congratulations, Charles. Go ahead, take her. I told ya you'd do well to join up with us."

Charles grabbed Ellie's arm, pulled her away from Spencer, and started leading her into the bedroom.

A sickened look on his face, Spencer said, "You boys are goin' to hell when you die, and you'll die soon because Judge Parker will be waitin' for you if you don't get shot down like the mangy dogs you are! And it can't be soon enough for me! You better kill me before you leave, 'cause I'll come after you and hunt you down!"

Rufus said, "Be careful what you wish for, my friend."

He pointed his revolver at Spencer and shot him twice rapidly in the chest.

Ellie screamed.

And her husband fell dead, gushing blood.

Ellie ran at Rufus and started beating him with her fists in his chest, his arms, his face—anything she could hit—even the hand that held his smoking gun.

He punched her in the head, knocking her groggy, and she fell.

Rufus turned toward Charles and said, "Get on with it, Cousin. Drag her into the bedroom. Hurry up, I'm horny."

Grinning delightedly, Charles hauled Ellie to her feet. She cried and struggled, trying to pull away from him, as he forced her down a hall and into a bedroom. The rude little room had plank walls decorated with crocheted homilies and prints taken from copies of the *Ladies' Home Journal.*

Charles said, "Just do as I say and we'll let you live, honey. You're gonna enjoy this. Don't worry, I'm good at it. We start young with our squaws."

Like a rag doll, she sank down onto the bed sitting on her haunches, tears streaming down her face.

Charles shrugged and sat next to her, then roughly pushed her down onto the homemade patchwork quilt. Then he pulled his trousers down and started tugging at her bodice and forcing kisses upon her.

Then suddenly she reached behind the headboard and pulled out a hidden knife.

Consumed with lust, he was oblivious to the sudden danger he was in.

She began returning his kisses, acting passionate, as much as she could will herself to do so. Then she rolled over to get on top of him.

He smiled up at her, obviously believing he was greatly pleasing her.

She slit his throat.

Blood sprayed from his gashed-open neck, and he gurgled and died, but she didn't look down at him to make sure.

She dropped the bloody knife on the bed and ran as swiftly and quietly as she could, down the hall and out through a side door.

A couple minutes later, Rufus Buck walked down the hall toward the bedroom.

He called out, "Havin' fun, Cousin?"

He stepped across the threshold and saw Charles's bloody body and slit throat—and his eyes went wide and his mouth gaped open from the shock of it.

He staggered backwards against a wall and screamed, "You fuckin' *bitch!*"

———

MEANTIME, in a valley between some rocky hills, Heck Thomas and Paden Tolbert were traveling slowly on their mounts, still tracking Rufus and his gang.

They looked up and halted when they saw about twenty armed riders looking down at them from a high ridge. The riders were silhouetted, and the two lawmen cupped their hands and shielded their eyes, trying to make them out.

Heck perked up and said, "I'll be damned! It's George Maledon up there with what looks to be a posse!"

"How d'you know it's George?" Paden said.

"Can't you see his stovepipe hat? Let's keep goin', they'll prob'ly come down here."

Within a few moments, Maledon and his posse rode down into the valley, and Maledon came forward with two other lawmen wearing the blue uniforms of the Indian Police.

Heck said, "Never thought we'd see you out here, George! What's goin' on?"

Grimly, Maledon said, "Sad to say, Sam Sixkiller and his wife were both murdered. And Rufus Buck did it. Took 'em totally unawares at a drugstore."

"Where?"

"In Muskogee. We know Rufus and his gang generally go running to his protectors in the Creek Nation, and we're hoping to catch up with him in time to avoid gunfire among the women and children. Don't want another Wounded Knee on our hands."

Heck said, "Well, maybe you guys don't know this yet, but they killed a lot of people at the Army Trading Station, and we think that young girl, Jolene Palmer, is still being held by them."

Maledon said, "Rufus might think he'll be protected by his fellow tribesmen, but that ain't gonna happen. Sam Sixkiller was a Creek, and highly thought of. The tribal elders want Rufus and his cronies gunned down or hanged. That's why they sent me a detachment of the Creek Lighthorse Police. These two guys are in charge of 'em. Meet Captain Edmund and Marshal Haynes."

Heck touched his right hand to his hat brim and said, "My name's Heck Thomas."

"We know," Captain Edmund said.

Paden said, "I've heard of you, Captain. My name's Paden Tolbert."

"Heard of you, too," said Captain Edmund.

George Maledon said, "Okay. We've got a job to do. So let's do it."

————

ELLIE DESPERATELY RAN toward the gang's horses and their wagon, not far from the house.

She stopped in her tracks, made a quick decision, jumped onto the seat of the wagon and took the reins, whipping them.

"C'mon, boy! Giddyup!"

The wagon lurched out and Ellie glanced back toward the house and saw Rufus, Sam, Lewis and Lukey starting to come after her. She whipped the reins harder, and the wagon picked up speed.

Rufus, Lewis, Sam and Lukey ran toward their horses.

Ellie drove the horse and wagon as hard as she could, down the dusty road and into a field of corn.

The corn was so high that it hid the whole wagon once she got in there. She drove the rig deep into a portion of the cornfield, then jumped down and started to run down one of the rows.

But she heard something that stopped her. It was Jolene's frantic, pleading voice.

"Please...help me...don't leave me..."

Ellie came closer to the wagon and peeled aside a corner of the tarp. She was jolted by the sight of the young girl being held prisoner in a cage. In spite of the fact that she could hear the men's galloping horses in the near distance, the undid the rawhide bindings of the tarp and the cage and set Jolene free, helping her down to the ground.

Ellie yelled, "C'mon! Hurry!"

And they both fled deeper into the cornfield.

———

RUFUS AND THE others rode up and dismounted at the edge of the crop-laden field. They could see wagon tracks going in.

Rufus snickered in anticipated triumph and motioned the three others to dismount, then did so himself. He waved them into the tall corn, using the wagon tracks as an indicator of where to pursue. But the early indicator soon petered out, and they could make out no other signs among the tall, thickly planted cornstalks.

Ellie and Jolene cowered in their hiding place.

Pistols drawn, Rufus and the boys prowled among the corn rows.

The women suppressed a gasp and desperately held their breath when Rufus passed within several feet of where they were concealed.

For about twenty minutes or so, which seemed like a long, boring time to them, the vicious teenagers prowled on the hunt. But they were impetuously and vacuously evil, not smart and persistent, and patience was not one of their hallmarks.

They started to tire of the chase. One by one, they straggled back out to the dirt road, and Rufus took his hat off and wiped his sweaty brow.

The others did the same.

Rufus said, "Let's get the hell outta this damn cornfield. It's too damn dusty and dry. My throat's cryin' for a drink of whisky."

Sam said, "Hell, yes! Me, too, Rufus."

Lewis scratched his head, nonplussed. "You gonna just let 'em go and tell on us? And what about the money we was gonna get for Jolene, from Peta Nocona?"

Rufus said, "Who they gonna tell? Way out here? Nearest town is more'n twenty miles. And how's the likes of Sam Sixkiller gonna be a problem with his throat slit? We won't see the likes of him ever again."

Listening to all this, Ellie and Jolene cowered in their hiding place, not daring to move or make a sound.

Lukey said, "We're givin' up a ton of money."

"Not necessarily," Rufus said. "Peta Nocona ain't goin' no place. We can capture another young girl that he'll like as much as Jolene, maybe more. That'll be our next mission. The horny old bastard has had so many of 'em he can't remember their faces. Long as they're young enough, he don't care."

Lukey said, "Well, screw it then. Let's go back to the Patterson's house and ransack it. Might be a lotta shit we can sell."

"Damn straight," Rufus said.

They all mounted up again, and Ellie and Jolene waited and listened to them leaving.

Ellie put her hand over Jolene's mouth and spoke in a hushed whisper. "Don't move yet, honey. It might be a trick. Let's make sure they're really gone."

They listened hard to the trotting hooves as the hoof beats slowly diminished. Then they dared to whisper.

Ellie confided, "They killed my husband. And they were going to rape me, all of them. Why did they have you in a cage?"

Jolene said, "I've been their prisoner for days. I think

they were going to sell me to some old Indian who has a lot of money somehow and likes young girls."

They kept listening for the hoof beats till they seemed to totally stop.

Then Ellie said, "Do you want to take a chance?"

With a tremble, Jolene nodded her assent.

They crouched low and started to warily creep out of the cornfield.

———

RUFUS AND LUKEY lounged on the front porch with a bottle of whisky that they passed back and forth. Then Sam and Lewis came out the front door carrying pillow cases filled with swag.

"We cleaned the place out," Sam said, "and we didn't get shit. Just trinkets mostly, but we took it all."

Lewis said, "Charles is a bloody mess. I covered him up, couldn't stand his wide-open eyes lookin' at me while we was grabbin' stuff in there."

"You're too finicky," Rufus said. "A corpse ain't gonna hurt you."

"But he's your cousin."

"He was. But he ain't no more. One thing is that he had a lifetime full of fun by comin' with us for the past few days."

"Yeah, his soul can rest easy on that," Lukey added with a short laugh.

Lewis and Sam laid their pillow sacks full of loot on the porch and Sam said, "Let me have a swig."

Lukey handed him the bottle, and he gulped some, then handed it to Lewis.

Lukey said, "We gonna hang around here for a while?"

Rufus said, "I dunno. At least there's food we can fry up. And we're pretty safe till someone comes snoopin'. And that ain't likely on these remote farms. I wouldn't mind sackin' out here instead of on the cold ground again."

"I got an itch," Lukey said, grinning slyly. "I'm thinkin' of going back into that cornfield."

"You shittin' me?" Sam slurred.

"I'd still like to poke Jolene. And it don't matter what I do to her now that we're not holdin' her for someone else. Fuck Peta Nocona and the horse he rode in on. Jolene might be thinkin' she's safe now and mighta crawled outta her hole. I might find her pretty easy."

Rufus said, "If you find 'em, kill 'em both when you're done with 'em."

"What I like to hear," said Lukey, and headed for his horse.

———

HECK THOMAS and Paden Tolbert were now part of the posse headed by George Maledon, Captain Edmund and Marshal Haynes. The band of over two dozen men headed out of the valley where they all met up and onto another stretch of dirt road and wooded hills. Within less than twenty more minutes, they came to the outskirts of the cornfield where Ellie Patterson and Jolene Palmer had been hiding.

Hearing the large group of men approaching, Ellie and Jolene peeked out from a row of corn. They were still badly frightened and didn't know if they could trust the newcomers. But when Ellie's eyes focused on the rider wearing the stovepipe hat, she became less wary, but still kept her voice to a whisper.

"I believe that man with the tall hat is George Maledon," she excitedly told Jolene. "I've seen him in Fort Smith, side by side with Judge Parker, going into a cigar shop. Everybody was in awe of them and pointing them out. We can show ourselves, Jolene!"

They stepped out from the corn row and hurried to the road.

Ellie cried out, "George! *George! Mr. Maledon!*"

George turned in his saddle, his eyes lit up and he said, "Oh-oh! What in the *world* have we stumbled into?" He was so glad that something was seeming to turn out right that he was at a loss for any further words.

Heck Thomas said, "We been tryin' to find you, Jolene. Your brother is alive and well and we're gonna take you to him."

Jolene and Ellie started babbling unintelligibly because of their high-strung emotions, but the ugly details of what was done to them stuck out in a way that was utterly shocking and almost made the lawmen's stomachs turn.

"Calm down, calm down, ladies," Captain Edmund said. "Where are they now? We've gotta catch up with them while we have a chance. We can't let those animals get away from us now that we know they ain't far. But we'll make sure you're safe."

"We won't be safe as long as they're anywhere around here!" Ellie said vehemently.

Jolene pleaded, "Please don't leave us here. They'll find us."

"Don't worry," the captain said. "I'm gonna assign four of my men to take you to Fort Smith, where you'll be under the protection of Judge Parker."

George Maledon said, "It's the safest place you can be

right now. Your brother is living with your grandparents, Jolene. He's been worrying and worrying about you."

"Ellie, do you have any friends or relatives at Fort Smith?" Heck asked. "Anybody who can take you in till the gang is put down?"

Ellie got a determined look on her face and said, "I don't want to go to Fort Smith. Give me a gun."

"You're kiddin'!" Heck exclaimed.

Unflinchingly, Ellie said, "They killed my husband. I know how to shoot. I'm used to baggin' squirrels and such. Give me a gun."

"Me, too," Jolene said, equaling Ellie with intensity.

"Well, we got a couple spare horses," Captain Edmund said to Heck and George.

"Give 'em to these ladies and *let's go!*" Heck shouted. "We're wastin' time, goddamn it!"

———

LUKEY DAVIS WAS APPROACHING the cornfield—and when he spied the posse, he kept his horse to one side of the road and around a tight bend where he could stay partly hidden. Scared by the imminent danger to himself, he watched Ellie and Jolene talking with the posse men. He couldn't hear what they were saying, but he didn't need to. It had struck him like a hammer blow that he and the rest of the gang were now in imminent danger. He turned his horse and guided it through rows of tall corn, forsaking the road. He went slowly among the cornstalks for a while, hoping he was concealed enough that he wouldn't attract the attention of the posse. Then he cut back out onto the dirt road, dug his spurs in and went faster.

Rufus was on the porch of the Pattersons' house with

Sam and Lewis when Lukey rode up in a gallop. "There's a big posse comin'!" Lukey shouted. "They're right down the road, and they're talkin' to the two women!"

Rufus said, "Damn! We've gotta outrun them! *C'mon!*"

Lukey's horse pranced in panicked circles as his cronies ran for their horses and got mounted. They charged off, and by this time the posse had appeared about four hundred yards down the road, and charged after them.

Above the clatter of hooves, Lukey shouted, "We ain't gonna outrun 'em! We got no chance! We shoulda made our stand right where we were!"

"No good! They'd've burned us out!" Rufus yelled back at him.

They pictured the Pattersons' house being hit by torches or dynamite and going up in flames like a pile of kindling, with them and their gang burnt to cinders in the conflagration.

They whipped their reins and spurred their mounts in a frenzy.

Rufus spied a steep, rocky slope and forced his horse to start climbing it. "C'mon!" he yelled—and the rest of the gang followed him.

It was a hard, perilous climb for the horses. Their hooves sent stones clattering as they climbed the steep incline, urged onward by the digging of spurs and the frantic whipping of their reins.

The gang made the peak in a wild scramble, jumped off of their mounts without bothering to tether them, yanking Winchesters from their saddle holsters and taking up firing positions behind huge boulders.

The leaders of the posse—George Maledon, Heck Thomas, Captain Edmunds and Marshal Haynes—thundered onto the path below, and the outlaws started blasting at them. The lawmen wheeled their horses and searched for cover. None of them were hit by the opening volley, and they left their horses to one side of the road as they fled to the protection of trees, bushes, logs or bushes close to the edge of the woods.

The firing of weapons from the top of the hill pursued them, but again nobody was hit.

"Ain't such good shots *are* they!" Maledon called out.

"Just don't go steppin' back out onto the road!" Heck told him. "Even a blind pig can get an acorn!"

Captain Edmund yelled at twenty or so of his men who were riding up to join the fray.

"Dismount, men! Protect your horses!"

They led their mounts into the surrounding woods and got them tethered.

The four leaders—Captain Edmund, Marshal Haynes, Heck Thomas and George Maledon—hunkered down together in a little ravine.

Ellie and Jolene arrived late, going slower than the rest of the posse on the mounts that were given them, but they did have rifles in their saddle sheathes. They dismounted and grabbed their Winchesters.

"Get *down!*" Heck yelled.

Both Jolene and Ellie dove for cover behind a fallen-down log fence. Bullets nicked the branches too close for comfort.

Captain Edmund and Marshal Haynes opened up with covering fire—and Rufus and Lukey ducked back behind some boulders as stone chips flew at their faces.

Heck and George took some potshots, but their bullets went astray.

Jolene and Ellie stuck their heads up and fired their

rifles, to no effect. The boulders up there on the hill were good protection, and the outlaws were too dug in.

Heck said to Maledon, "We've gotta protect ourselves and the ladies, too, and the best way of doin' that is to keep the sons-of-bitches pinned down up there."

Captain Edmund said, "I agree. Even if they have a rifle and two revolvers apiece, that would amount to about thirty rounds each. Sooner or later they'll run outta ammo."

George said, "As long as none of us get killed in the meantime."

A fusillade erupted from up on the slope, followed by overlapping return fire from the lawmen and the two women. Chunks flew from the trunks of trees protecting the people below, and chips flew from the rocks concealing the outlaws.

It seemed like a pretty solid standoff.

Captain Edmund called out in a low, hoarse voice to Heck, George and Marshal Haynes. "How much ammo can they have with 'em? If we keep suckerin' 'em into shootin' at us while we're hunkered down, they'll prob'ly soon run out of bullets."

"We already agreed with ya on that," Heck said.

Captain Edmund rose partway up and shouted at the posse. "Listen up, men! Fire on my command!"

There was a clatter of rifles and pistols being cocked.

Then, "One, two, three...*fire!*"

The whole posse cut loose, and it was a deafening fusillade for a short while, then it got quieter as men had to reload.

As predicted, the gang on the hill responded by shooting like mad, even though none of the posse members were exposed enough to be easily hit.

"Dumb fucks, *ain't* they?" George Maledon said.

"Just keep your head down" said Heck.

"Well, I'm just sayin' they ain't the brightest no-good bastards on the planet," Maledon persisted.

Marshal Haynes said, "I'm amazed nobody's been hit. My men are all good shots."

"Yeah, but their bullets can't go through boulders," said Captain Edmunds said with consternation. "And even if the ones up there ain't the best, if this goes on and on, they'll get lucky."

Heck said, "Any way somebody could sneak around and get behind 'em?"

Marshal Haynes said, "Like who?"

"Like me. I might be able to do it. I've done it in similar situations."

George said, "I told ya you should be in the dime novels."

Captain Edmunds said, "There ain't no way up there from the other side. It's a sheer cliff. No way up and no way down."

"Then they're between a rock and a hard place," said Maledon, smirking.

"Well, I'll be, the hangman has a sense of humor," said Captain Edmunds.

Another fusillade broke out from up on the rocks, and the lawmen ducked and hid.

Ellie and Jolene stuck their heads up and fired back, then ducked down. Again they were almost grazed by bullets.

When things quieted down, Heck and George dared to take peek. And when they saw Rufus and Lukey sticking their heads up and poking their rifles out, they fired at them. But they missed narrowly—their bullets driving rock splinters into the outlaws' faces.

Heck and George ducked back down.

The outlaws started blasting away again.

Captain Edmunds said, "Good. Very good. Let them blow their wad."

But they stopped shooting.

Up on top of the hill, Lukey said, "We're gonna run outta ammo, and they prob'ly know it, Rufus."

Sam was close by, and he said, "I still have six rounds in one of my Colts and half a magazine in my Winchester."

Lewis said, "I'm about in the same shape."

Lukey said, "Me, too. What if we draw straws, pick two of us to keep 'em pinned while the other two slip away, down the other side of this slope?"

"Can't go down the back side, it's a sheer drop," Sam said.

Lewis said, "How about only *one* of us keeps 'em pinned down while *three* of us get away, and I wouldn't mind bein' one of the three."

"Tell you the truth," Rufus squelched, "I don't think any of us are gonna get away. I think this is our last stand and we better make it a good one. We all knew it'd come to this by and by. Too many odds against us, been that way all our lives. At least we had a damn good run at it, boys. If we had a bottle of whisky up here, I'd damn sure toast to it."

"You sayin' you're ready to cash in?" Lukey said disbelievingly.

"I'm just sayin' we prob'ly don't have much choice. We prob'ly gotta throw ourselves on the mercy of the damned posse."

In a slow, sad drawl, Sam said, "We could do like Custer did, if we wanna be heroes."

As if it didn't matter to him one way or another, he

took a bag of tobacco out of his jacket pocket and put a pinch under his tongue.

Lukey angrily spat a thick wad of spittle onto the dusty ground and said, "What the fuck did Custer do that was so fuckin' great? My uncle was at Little Big Horn, and it was a goddamn great victory for our people. They called that sucker Yellow Hair, and all the warriors was dyin' to scalp him, but they couldn't find his body. They split outta there yellin' and whoopin', Crazy Horse and the rest of 'em, and Geronimo made a painting about in on a big piece of leather."

Sam drawled, "What I'm sayin' is that Custer and his men fought to the bitter end. But they kept their last bullet for their own selves. When they couldn't do no more they blew their brains out."

Rufus said, "The bluebellies knew they'd be tortured if they let themselves be captured. They wasn't brave. They just didn't have the guts to face torture."

"Would you?" Lewis challenged.

"I won't have to find out, smartass.! The whites ain't gonna torture us. They like to think they're more goddamned *civilized* than we are!"

"So what will they do?" Sam asked.

"Put us on trial. We'll get to defend ourselves and let the whole world know why we did what we did. We might not even get the death sentence, the whites on the jury might be too damn softhearted."

Lukey said, "Dream on. They're gonna hang us."

Down below, the lawmen were biding their time.

Captain Edmund said, "Awful quiet for a long while. Maybe their ammo give out already."

Suddenly Marshal Haynes exclaimed, "Hot diggity! Look!"

Up in the rocks, a stick poked up with a dirty rag on it.

"I'll be damned!" Heck said.

Captain Edmund cupped his hand around his mouth and yelled, "Hey, up there! You wanna surrender, stand up and let us see ya! Hands up! And without no weapons!"

Lukey stuck his head up a little bit. He was the one waving the dirty white rag. Still scared, he yelled, "We ain't fools! You'll gun us down!"

Captain Edmund yelled back, "That's the chance you'll have to take! But I give you my word!"

All the posse members watched with nervous anticipation.

Jolene and Ellie stared upwards with shaky looks on their faces.

A couple of the gang members peeked out from the rocks, then they emerged warily and started scrambling down the hill, trying to keep their hands up instead of using them for balance.

Sam and Lewis fell on their butts and had to scramble back up.

They finally got down to where the posse was and—surprise!—Rufus Buck wasn't with them. Only Sam, Lewis and Lukey had come down off the hill.

Captain Edmund, George Maledon, and Marshal Haynes stepped forward, pistols trained on the three murderers.

George said, "Where the hell is Rufus? Is he dead? Did one of our bullets nail him?"

Lukey grinned. "Hell no, he ain't dead! He's got nine lives! You go up there, you're gonna see a rope tied to a tree and the rest of it dangled down the cliff. He's long gone, man! You ain't never gonna catch up to him!"

As handcuffs were being put on Lukey, Sam and Lewis, they cast evil, triumphant looks at the lawmen and burst into a chorus of hoarse laughs.

But Heck Thomas was so angry that he said, "I'm going up there, George. He ain't gonna get away so easy. I'm gonna go after him."

George said, "He's a slick bastard, I'll give him that. But I ain't climbin' no rocks with my lumbago. We'll keep a close eye on these other assholes while you're gone."

As Heck started his climb, with his pistol drawn, the posse guys herded the three captured gang members toward a flat-bedded wagon and started shackling them to the wagon's rails.

Ellie and Jolene were still together at the edge of the woods, and they eyed the killers with pure hatred.

Ellie trembled and bit her lip. She raised her rifle, seated the butt of it tightly into her right shoulder, and took dead aim at Lukey's chest.

But suddenly her rifle was yanked away—by Marshal Haynes.

He said, "You don't wanna do that, honey. You'd be up for murder. And you know damn well that Judge Parker would follow the letter of the law."

Ellie burst into tears, and Jolene put her arms around her while she cried her eyes out.

Heck made it to the top of the hill and warily looked all around. It was dead quiet. Nothing seemed to be moving.

Then he saw the tree with the rope tied to it, and he moved toward it.

True to Lukey's words, the rope was dangling over the edge of the cliff, all the way to the ground. Heck peered downward, but the brush down there appeared undisturbed.

Then he heard a scraping sound—from behind him. And Rufus Buck popped up and fired his Winchester.

Heck dove—and Rufus's bullet went wild.

Heck hit the ground and rolled over, at the same time returning fire from down on the ground—and Rufus took a bullet in his shoulder and his rifle went flying.

Heck ran up to Rufus as he was trying to use his good arm to get his pistol out of its holster. He managed to do it just as Heck got up close to him—and Rufus pulled his trigger.

But he only got a click—no more ammo.

Heck kicked the pistol out of Rufus's hand and pointed his own Colt revolver at Rufus's head.

Rufus was flat on his back, squirming and crying with the pain of his blood-soaked shoulder. He wailed, "Go ahead, you son-of-a-bitch! Shoot me and get it over with!"

Heck said, "I never kick a man when he's down, but this time I'll make an exception."

He kicked Rufus twice, really hard, in his leg and in his chest.

Rufus cried out in severe pain.

Heck said, "What's the matter, you big baby? You can dish it out, but you can't take it?"

"Fuck you," Rufus said.

25

H ANG 'EM! HANG 'EM! HANG 'EM!

Captain Edmund stared at the rowdy crowd through a barred window of the Muskogee Jail. There were at least fifty people out there of all racial mixtures. If their mood turned uglier, they might storm the jail and string the outlaws up. The captain knew first-hand what could happen when a mob turned ugly. In the 1860's after serving on the Union side during the Civil War, he was working for the Pinkerton Detective Agency and helped track down and arrest the notorious Reno Brothers Gang in Canada and take them in chains to New Albany, Indiana, where they were to be tried for a slew of kidnappings, tortures and murders. But that night, five uniformed policemen were overpowered by dozens of vigilantes who used a battering ram to break down the heavy front doors of the jail. Newspaper headlines called it the *Night of Blood*.

John Edmund wasn't there when it happened, but he heard the stories and witnessed the aftermath. When the five city policemen were questioned, they claimed that they were unable to identify any of the vigilantes because they were all wearing hats with the brims pulled down and scarlet masks with narrow eye-slits. The cops maintained it would've been useless to open fire on the crazed mob because they couldn't possibly have killed them all, or even most of them, before themselves being overwhelmed and possibly clubbed or shot to death. But John Edmund thought it more likely that they weren't about to risk their own lives to protect vicious, ruthless, much-hated outlaws.

The upshot was that the mob forced the jailers to hand over their keys. The cell doors were unlocked while the prisoners cowered in terror. Frank Reno was dragged out pleading and crying. A noose was slipped over his head, the other end was tied to a beam on a second-floor ceiling, and he was tossed over a balcony, screaming, and dropped hard as the rope jerked tight. With a loud snap, his neck broke. The vigilantes held up a lantern to watch his dead body swing. One of them yelled, "Get William Reno!"

A second cell door was swung open, and three men dragged William Reno out. He stammered incoherently, "Please...gentlemen...my father...oh, protect...my..." That's all his executioners could make out before the noose choked off his last words. He too was hurled over the second-floor rail. His body flopped and his eyes popped from his skull and he slowly strangled to death, swinging back and forth in little circles.

But Simeon Reno did not go as easily. He wrenched the iron sink from the wall of his cell and used one of its iron legs as a club. He managed to bash three of the vigilantes, injuring them badly but not fatally, before he was beaten to the floor, tied up and hanged.

Another gang member, Charlie Anderson, begged and

wept as the vigilantes dragged him out. With the noose around his neck, they tossed him high into the air, but the rope tore in two, and he sprawled on the floor screaming and babbling. They pulled him to his feet and put a second noose over his head. Then they lowered him and let him slowly strangle to death.

Scowling at prisoners in the other cells who had not belonged to the Reno gang, one of the vigilantes cried out, "Let's hang 'em all!"

But their leader said, "No. We did what we came here for. Now we'll go."

They left four hanged bodies twisting in their wake.

But the prisoners who had been spared were horrified as Simeon Reno seemingly came back to life. His bulging eyes popped open and he began jerking at the end of the rope like a hooked fish. Some of men still locked in their cells watched in wretched fascination as his body swayed back and forth, his toes barely touching the stone floor, as he died by inches.

The Night of Blood was over.

But it wasn't over in Captain John Edmund's mind even though he had not witnessed it in person and could have done nothing to prevent it. The testimony of the cops who had been there and their surviving prisoners had burned itself into his brain permanently. He desperately did not want another vigilante episode like that on his watch.

The frenzied crowd outside was chanting: STRING 'EM UP! STRING 'EM UP!

Captain Edmund shook his head in consternation as he turned toward the cells where Rufus Buck, Lukey Davis, Lewis Davis and Sam Sampson were being held. Rufus had a bandage on his shoulder and his right arm was in a sling.

The captain said, "There's damn near as many Creeks out there as there are white people. None of 'em are yellin' let 'em go, they all wanna hang y'all."

Sneeringly, Rufus said, "You gonna let 'em do it?"

"Naw, I'm too damn honorable."

Lukey said, "You could just let 'em break the door down and overpower you. Nobody could blame you for that, Captain. You might even get a medal."

Edmund was hit by irony of what Lukey just said because the callous suggestion echoed with stark images of the Night of Blood. It struck him that the officially sanctioned method used by Judge Parker and George Maledon to dispose of murderers and rapists was a way of cleaning it up, making it seem less vicious, less ugly, less brutal and more "civilized." But did that mean it was more justified? Captain Edmund couldn't answer that. He just knew that he didn't want to be the person applying the noose.

He heard heavy footsteps on the stoop then pounding on the heavy front door, and he had to peer out through the window bars to make sure of who it was.

George Maledon shouted through the glass, "Let us in afore this mob attacks us!"

Captain Edmund unbolted the door, and Heck Thomas and George Maledon barged in, the shouts of the angry mob suddenly louder till the door went shut. They were lugging a bag of sandwiches and big steaming pot with a ladle in it.

"Ham sandwiches and hot black coffee," Heck said. "There's enough for us and the prisoners."

Edmund said, "Might be the last meal they ever get, if that crowd out there has its way. Might be *our* last, too. What're we gonna do about it?"

Heck blinked, smiled drolly, and said, "We better go out and talk to 'em, right, George?"

Behind the bars of their cells, Rufus and the gang got a big, scoffing ha-ha out of that.

George Maledon said, "I ain't got nothin' to say to 'em."

"We have to calm them down somehow," Captain Edmund insisted. "I helped bring in the Ringo brothers and they didn't last the night out. I wasn't there when they were lynched, but it was a horrible sight afterwards. I don't wanna see anything like that ever again. Besides, we all swore an oath to uphold the law, which includes protecting prisoners."

Heck said, "I wanna try goin' out and talkin' to 'em. But I want George by my side with his shotgun."

George said, "If you get *me* shot I'll be pissed off."

Rufus got as close as he could get to the bars of his cell and said jeeringly, "I hope to hell you *both* get shot!"

Maledon picked up his double-barreled shotgun, pointed it in Rufus's direction and said, "Shut your damn mouth or my weapon might discharge accidentally."

Rufus let loose with one of his snickers.

Heck unbarred the door, and he and George stepped out.

Cries of HANG 'EM! and HAND 'EM OVER! filled the air. But Heck ignored the ruckus and started to speak. As loud as he could, he yelled, "Listen up, people! You want justice and you want it right now! But that ain't the way the law works!"

One of the mob's obvious leaders was a man wearing bright green suspenders and a green bowler hat. He had a pistol in his right hand and a coil of rope in his other hand, and he blurted, "The law *don't* work! But a rope *does!*"

Heck said, "Well, I guarantee you that the law damn well *will* work! All of you might not recognize this fellow standin' next to me, but he's George Maledon, Judge Parker's main man for dispensing justice! He and I worked hard to help Captain Edmund hunt these desperadoes down, and we aim to see it through! We'll be takin' 'em to Fort Smith tomorrow to face Judge Parker in court! And anybody that tries to stop us might find themselves gettin' the same kinda punishment that these lawbreakers surely will!"

The crowd mumbled and complained, but their anger seemed to subside a bit.

Heck said, "My advice to y'all is to go home right now, and tomorrow at noon you can watch us put 'em on the train to the gallows! Y'all liked and admired Sam Sixkiller and he was a man who honored the law. The best way to honor his memory and his wife's memory is to let the law work the way he would've wanted it to!"

After some more mumbling and sporadic outbursts, the crowd subsided to murmurs and slowly started to disperse.

When the mob had thinned out enough to seem as though they had lost their bravado, Heck and George ducked back inside the jail.

Captain Edmund bolted the door and said with an attempt at wry humor, "Nice job, but it took too long. I hope you like cold coffee."

George said, "Very funny, Captain."

Rufus and his fellow prisoners let loose with a burst of mocking laughter.

Captain Edmund turned to Heck and asked, "Why'd you tell that mob the prisoners'll be on the noon train?"

"Because they're gonna be on the *six A.M.* train. Hopefully we can sneak 'em outta here before any sizable mob forms up. How many of your men can we have as an armed escort at dawn?"

Captain Edmund said, "Marshal Haynes is gonna be here tomorrow. It's too late to round up another posse."

Heck said, "The four of us will have to handle it, then."

He pulled a ham sandwich out of the bag, took a bite of it, faced the prisoners' cells and spoke matter-of-factly. "You boys are gonna have to cooperate to save your own skins. We don't want to have to face down another mob tomorrow morning, and we don't dare unchain you. So you're gonna have to pick up your chains and walk down to the train station carrying them. The whole town will come awake and realize what's happening if they hear you clanking and rattling, and if that happens we won't necessarily be able to stave them off, and you'll get lynched."

Rufus said, "A lot you care, you son-of-a-bitch! Now let me have my goddamn ham sandwich!"

———

AN HOUR before the first light of dawn, the main part of Muskogee consisted of shut-down shops and empty streets.

Armed with pistols and shotguns, Heck Thomas and George Maledon came out of the jail first, to stand guard while Captain Edmund and Marshal Haynes herded Rufus and his gang of miscreants outside, in chains. Then, with two lawmen stepping along briskly on either side of them, the captives were escorted through the little town, holding their chains in their arms to keep them from clanking as they trudged along, looking wary and scared, as if nooses were going to suddenly appear in the sky.

A couple of early risers came out of shops or houses, shaking their heads and staring.

The man in the bowler hat and green suspenders, who last night had acted so bravely as the head of a mob, was now a drunk, sleeping in an alley. He sat up and wiped his eyes groggily, and seemed to disbelieve what he was seeing. Heck and George gave each other looks of relief that the blowhard who used to be so blustery was lying there in a drunken stupor and didn't have his pistol and his coil of rope anymore.

After a long, suspenseful trudge, the murderers and their armed escort managed to arrive at the train depot without incident. The prisoners dropped their chains in the dirt, not caring anymore how much noise they made. They grumbled and cursed, and stretched and twisted, attempting to relieve their aching arm and back muscles.

In a short while, the train came in, chugging and hissing, and the chained-up prisoners were prodded into a boxcar, with more cursing and grumbling. The four heavily armed lawmen got in with them with weapons steadily pointed at the gang's chests.

But at Fort Smith a huge rowdy crowd, much larger and more vociferous than the mob at Muskogee, was anxiously awaiting the arrival of the Rufus Buck gang. Hundreds of people were there to greet the train, and they were all in a foul mood. The train pulled in at the platform, the door of the boxcar slid open, and the four lawmen were stunned when they looked out and their eyes got used to a blast of stark sunlight.

Captain Edmund said, "Holy shit!"

George Maledon said, "I agree."

Somebody yelled, "They're here! The filthy animals!"

Somebody else yelled, "They don't deserve a trial!"

The prisoners were instantly so scared that they didn't get to their feet to descend from the boxcar. They looked like they just wanted to stay in there and hope the train would somehow start rolling again with them in it.

A rough, loud voice bellowed, "I'd like to chop 'em up and feed 'em to my hogs!"

Somebody else said, "Your hogs might be able to stomach 'em, but I *can't!*"

The mob started chanting: STRING 'EM UP! STRING 'EM UP!

Heck Thomas, George Maledon, Captain Edmund and Marshal Haynes slowly, almost reluctantly, stepped out of the boxcar and waved shotgun barrels at the outlaws to make them get out.

George Maledon was surprised to see Ellie Patterson, Tommy Palmer and his sister, Jolene, standing together, arms around each other, at the edge of the train platform. They were clapping and jeering along with the rest of the crowd when the four captives were herded out of the boxcar and onto the platform.

Rufus sneered and jammed his middle finger at all of the people, lifting his heavy chain and the shackle on his left wrist to do so. He couldn't do it with his right hand because that arm was in a sling.

The obscene gesture provoked the crowd so much that they started charging forward.

"We're in deep shit, Heck!" Maledon cried out.

But suddenly they heard a heavy trudge of marching boots and a sergeant barking commands—and to their great relief a platoon of Fort Smith soldiers came marching down to the train platform, forcing the crowd to part.

Maledon said, "Saved, by God!"

And Rufus blurted, "Fuck 'em all!"

A church bell started to toll. It overrode the noise of the crowd and the chugging of the train and hissing of steam as it left the station.

Heck said, "That bell is tolling for your victims, Rufus. You better start praying and begging for mercy in the afterlife 'cause you ain't gonna get none down here on God's earth."

———

AFTER DELIVERING their prisoners to the soldiers who would take them to the Fort Pitt jail, George Maledon excused himself from the other lawmen and reported to Judge Parker about how the mood of the populace not just in Fort Smith but also in Muskogee had been teetering on the very edge of violence.

"I would've expected no less," the judge said when they once again met in his chambers. "We'll need to be ready to control an outbreak at every second of the trial, and that's why I want to get it over with as expeditiously as possible. I want it to be fair, but expeditious."

"Understood, sir," George Maledon acknowledged.

"I've had several comprehensive meetings with the prosecutor and the defense counsel. Nobody wanted to defend the culprits, they didn't want to have anything to do with the case, for fear of reprisals. But I finally found somebody who relented, albeit it shakily. We agreed on principles upon which the judicial details will proceed. We see no need for the young Palmer girl to be involved. The experience would be too devastating for her, on top of all that she has already been forced to go through."

After a further discussion of these points, George took a street car to a saloon where he, Heck Thomas,

Captain Edmund and Marshal Haynes had agreed to unwind from the stress of delivering the prisoners. They sat together at a table where they were supplied with draft beer, two bottles of whisky and the accompanying shot glasses.

They talked about the fact that the ragtag Rufus Buck gang, a bunch of stupid and recklessly brutal teenagers, had managed to kill two wary and highly experienced agents of the law, Sheriff John Garrett and Captain Sam Sixkiller.

George said, "None of us can protect ourselves totally in all circumstances. It's one thing to go up against a gunslinger face to face. But any determined renegade can sneak up on us if he's a mind to put a bullet or two in our backs."

"Rufus Buck and his bunch were emboldened when they got the jump on John Garrett," Heck said. "After that, they thought they were invincible."

"Nah, they always knew they'd get caught," Marshal Haynes contradicted. "They just didn't care anymore about consequences. They're too damn dumb. No imagination. Nothing to live for, in their own minds. So they enjoyed their spree of lawlessness for as long as they could, and the world be damned."

"Look at this headline in yesterday's *Daily News Record*," Captain Edmund said, holding up a folded newspaper. "*Thirteen Days of Terror!* Nine killings and eight gang rapes in less than two weeks! The editorial says they shouldn't be glorified or romanticized like the Daltons or the James boys, they're just mindless murderers and rapists, utterly heinous and depraved, and that's what makes 'em so terrifying."

"I get 'em on my scaffold, they won't terrify nobody

no more," George Maledon said with utter certainty, and tossed down a slug of whisky as punctuation.

Heck thought that one over. "I think the horror they caused will stick to 'em long after they're dead. They'll keep haunting people's dreams, like the Boogey Man or somethin', human beings who turned into monsters."

"I guess we're sort of the killers of monsters, then," Captain Edmund said with a wry grimace. "That's the role we've accepted in our society."

"That's the role that's been *thrust* on us," said Major Haynes.

"Nothin' to do but drink to it," said George Maledon. And he tossed down another slug of whisky. Then he said, "Thank God neither Tommy Palmer nor his sister Jolene will have to testify in court. That's what Judge Parker told me."

"Why not?" Heck asked. "Tommy saw them lynch his father, and Jolene saw them rape and kill her mother. The death penalty would be a sure thing."

"The prosecutor has decided that the first thing on his agenda will be to try the whole gang for the rape of Mrs. Rosetta Hansen. It was horrible, and it carries the death penalty just like murder does. It was one of the first crimes they committed at the start of their rampage. Mighta happened even before they killed Johnny Garrett."

Captain Edmund said, "Lots of people think rape is *worse* than murder. Let's hope that goes for whoever's on their jury."

Marshal Haynes pursed his lips and shook his head. He said, "I don't believe there's a chance in hell for a not guilty verdict or even a mistrial. Whites and Indians alike want Rufus Buck and the rest of the scumbags dead, and they'd weave the rope or strangle them with their bare hands if they had to."

"Yeah," said Captain Edmund. "Lots of folks, back east especially, wanna believe that the West is more civilized by now, but the shit Rufus Buck and them did rips the mask off of the worst side of human nature. People don't like to face it that that kind of depravity might exist in all of us and might show its ugly face under the right circumstances. They're not going to easily forgive."

"In other words, they're gonna wipe the ugliness away with a vengeance," said George Maledon. "I'm gonna work on my ropes and knots, get 'em good and ready."

————

THAT SAME AFTERNOON, Judge Parker sat in alone in his chambers and wrote a eulogy for Sam Sixkiller, whose funeral was coming up two days ahead, on a Sunday. The piece that the judge wrote under lamented the death of Sam's wife, Fannie, and praised Captain Sixkiller for his heroism and courage. He intended to read from it during the services, and it would then be published in the *Daily Record*.

"The captain did more than any one person to free the railroad towns of this territory of their dangerous and reckless elements. All of our peaceful and productive citizens are indebted to him for the comparative security of life and property that they have usually enjoyed. Captain Sam Sixkiller died a martyr to the cause of law and order and he rightfully earned and deserved the respect and confidence of all decent people. The Cherokee Nation can be proud of their hero and know that his shoes will be hard to fill by anyone of any race.

At the hands of murderous assassins, our esteemed friend has been taken from our midst, and all peoples must deeply deplore the cruel and untimely loss of a kindly, honorable man who bravely gave his all in the cause of peace and justice for all races."

Two days later, over two thousand mourners attended Captain Sixkiller's funeral, and the church could not contain them all. Their procession to the cemetery was a staggering testimony to the love and high regard which the people felt for Sam, and it also cemented the universal feeling that the Rufus Buck gang was not going to fare very well before a jury in Judge Isaac Parker's courtroom.

26

George Maledon was sound asleep and sweating in his clothes when he was awakened by somebody lightly tapping on his door. He sat up, still woozy from the liquor he had drunk at the saloon with the other three lawmen, and shambled to the door. When he opened it, Tommy Palmer was looking up at him.

"Mr. Maledon," the boy said shyly. "I have a favor I need to ask you."

"Well, spit it out," George said, not in a mean way, but in a manner that would encourage the boy to speak his mind.

Tommy said, "Mrs. Patterson…Ellie…asked Jolene to go with her to help pack up her clothes and stuff that she needs from her farmhouse…where her husband was killed. I said I'd go, too. She's gonna hire a wagon from the livery stable tomorrow to haul her things."

"How's she gonna have her husband buried?"

"That's gonna be done, too. Some of the men from the Creek Nation want to do it for her, to make up for what the gang done. They said they're embarrassed that some of their own young men, born and raised among them, went bad and did all those horrible deeds."

"Understandable," said George. "Some people say the only good Injun is a dead Injun, but that ain't true, and don't you forget it. Without the help of the Indian Police, we wouldn't have brought those darn killers to justice."

"But we're still scared to go back there by ourselves," Tommy said. "I mean at least the women are...not me so much."

"So you want me to go with you," he surmised.

He could tell that the boy was trying to sound a bit braver than he might actually be.

"Well...yes, sir. And do you think Heck Thomas or somebody would go with you?"

"I can certainly talk to him about it," George said.

————

AT DAWN THE NEXT MORNING, a larger group than what was first anticipated met at Heck and Mattie's house to set out for the Patterson farm. She insisted on coming along to help out and to pay her respects to Spencer, who had been one of her students in her younger days as a schoolmarm. She cooked a big breakfast of ham and eggs for all of them and they ate in her kitchen before they got started. Heck and George gulped their food down, then headed for the livery stable to get a horse-drawn wagon with a long bed and a double row of seats. There was plenty of room in the bed for the household stuff that Ellie wanted to take back with her.

Heck and George, on horseback, rode alongside of the wagon. Ellie and Jolene rode in the front seat with Ellie taking the reins, and Tommy and Mattie rode on the seat behind them. Luckily, the Patterson farm was only eighteen miles out of Fort Smith, so they figured that they could do everything in one day, even if they didn't get back till sundown.

In addition to cooking breakfast, Mattie had packed a huge lunch into a wicker basket with large chips of ice folded between layers of linen to keep everything from spoiling. It would have felt almost like going on a picnic or a camping trip if it weren't for the fact that they were going to be heading into a place where they had suffered anguish, torment and death. And those ungodly experiences were never far from their minds.

Surprisingly, Tommy, expressed a desire to see the rocky hill where the Rufus Buck gang had been pinned down till they surrendered, so that's where they stopped to have their lunch. He jumped down from the wagon almost before it stopped, excited and in awe over the place where the outlaws had made their last stand. The adults figured it was best to let the boy go, so he might be able to exorcise some of his demons by clothing them in reality. They didn't phrase it that way, but they knew what they felt without saying it.

It had been comfortably cool when they started out at sunrise, but now it was the hottest part of the day, hard to find a good spot to dig into the fried chicken, lemonade, ears of corn and homemade bread that Mattie had packed in the hamper. They remarked quite a few times that most of the ice had melted and the linen was soaked.

"Good," George Maledon said. "I want some to mop my brow with."

Following his lead, they each took one of the wet, cold linen cloths and wiped their faces and cooled their necks and brows.

Heck and George found a nearby stream back in the woods a ways and were able to water the horses.

As it turned out, the best place for them to have their lunch was in the spread-out area where the posse had taken refuge from the outlaws' fusillades. The women laid out the food and the drinks on a spread-out blanket, awkward to use because of the lumpy ground underneath.

Heck put his arm around Mattie's shoulder and kissed her to show how proud he was of her self-assuredness and her deep empathy for others. Usually he would've been too shy to kiss her in front of other people, but this time he couldn't help himself.

Tommy wouldn't eat anything right away. Instead he scrambled around hunting for spent cartridges and gathering them up and putting them into his bulging pockets. Then he ran around scrutinizing the rocks, trees and branches for bullet nicks or imbedded lead.

When he impetuously started climbing the steep, rocky hill across the dirt road from where the others were eating, Heck followed behind him to guard him from harm, in case there was anybody dangerous lurking up there. If any of the gang members had friends or relatives who mourned them and sympathized with them and resented the fact that they were obviously going to be hanged, such persons might come to this spot to sing their death song and vow eternal revenge on the "white devils."

No one was there when Heck and Tommy got to the top, but the rope was still tied to the tree and it was still dangling over the edge of the cliff, and Tommy stared at that for a long while, his blue eyes wide and his mouth working without comment.

156 | JOHN A. RUSSO

Then he asked Heck, "Where was Rufus Buck when you shot him?"

Heck tried to pick out the exact spot, but the blood had soaked into the ground and had been probably washed away by rain.

"Right about here," Heck said. "He tried to play me for a fool so he could kill me, but I got lucky."

"I think you're just a lot smarter'n he is," Tommy said. "And a better shot."

"I kicked him after I shot him," Heck admitted. "Don't tell Mattie, though."

"I won't. But I'm glad you did it."

Heck didn't respond to that because he wasn't sure how.

Tommy said, "I wish I was there. I'd have stomped on his neck."

Heck was taken aback by the boy's vehemence, but he said nothing.

They went back down the slope, the rocks skittering under their boots just like they had done when the outlaws and their horses scrambled up there out of desperation.

By that time, the ladies had the food and other stuff put away, what was left of it. And they were ready to move on to the Patterson place.

Things got more tense at that point, because this used to be a home that Ellie cherished, and now it was where her husband had been killed, she had almost been raped, and she had killed the young man who was going to do it to her. And if he had succeeded, the others would have piled on.

When they came down the road leading to the farm, the place seemed deadly quiet.

They pulled up in front and tethered the horses.

Nothing else was moving. George and Heck got down from their mounts and the others jumped down from the wagon.

They heard noises coming from the backyard. So they warily walked around the side of the house, and Heck and George didn't draw their pistols right away, but they felt an urge to. They stopped in their tracks when they saw two big men carrying a wooden coffin out through the back door. And they were surprised when they squinted into the sun and recognized the men as Captain Edmund and Marshal Haynes.

Heck said to Mattie, Jolene, Ellie and Tommy, "No need to be scared. We know those two men."

"So do I," said Ellie. "They came to me the other day and said they wanted to help me in my hour of need. I just didn't know they were coming here so soon."

They hastened their pace toward the end of the yard where there was a small family plot with five or six gravestones. And they saw that Spencer's grave was already dug, when Marshal Hayes and Captain Edmund set the coffin down beside it.

They all greeted each other with hugs and handshakes, and the captain said, "Some of our tribesmen made the coffin for you. And we just finished digging the grave."

Ellie was overwhelmed and started to cry.

Marshal Haynes said, "Some of our Cherokee women cleaned the house for you. The Cherokee Nation wants to show that none of us condone what Rufus Buck and his gang have done here."

"Thank you from the bottom of my heart," Ellie said, sobbing.

"We can lower your husband into the earth and say

our prayers for him anytime you're ready, Mrs. Patterson," said Captain Edmund.

"I can't thank you enough," Ellie said, and her tears wouldn't stop coming.

Jolene handed her a hanky and she kept dabbing at her eyes.

"Never expected to see you here today," George Maledon said to the two Cherokee policemen.

"We don't go around boasting about things we're gonna do for people," Captain Edmund said. "We're just glad to be able to do it."

"Can I just look at him for a final time?" Ellie asked.

"Sure, Ma'am," said the captain.

She knelt before the coffin and bowed her head. Then she arose and said, "You can close the coffin now, please, gentlemen."

The captain and the marshal put the heavy wooden lid on the coffin and nailed it shut. Then Heck Thomas and George Maledon helped them lower it into the grave, first sliding ropes under it and using the ropes to let the coffin descend slowly until it hit bottom.

They took turns shoveling till the grave was filled in, then patted down a final mound of dirt on top.

Major Edmund had brought a Christian Bible and was thumbing through it to find a suitable passage—when suddenly appeared a mass of people marching down the road, wailing in perfect unison some sort of Indian chant.

Heck and George were startled when they saw that the procession was being led by Peta Nocona. The same three young squaws that they had seen dying leather in a boiling cauldron were walking behind the medicine man with their heads bowed in absolute submission, an homage and an acceptance of their slavery, sexual and otherwise. And behind them came dozens of Cherokees presumably innocent of Peta's hypocrisy, all in traditional tribal regalia as they gathered closely around the white mourners, with their chanting unabated.

Standing next to Heck, George Maledon muttered in a low voice, "Look at that sly old bastard, Peta Nocona, pretending to be some kind of noble savage."

Heck said, "Try to be more charitable, George. He might have an ounce of good in him."

"An ounce would be about it, or maybe half an ounce," George derided. "I've got a hunch that Rufus Buck and his followers wouldn't have gone so hog-wild if it wasn't for him indoctrinating them."

Jolene overheard part of their whispers and rushed over to them, her face a mask of outraged emotion.

"Did I hear that name right?" she blurted. "Peta something? That's the old Indian that Rufus Buck was going to sell me to!"

The chanting was of such volume that no one heard what Jolene said except for Heck and George. And they didn't know what to say to Jolene's revelation.

"Can't he be arrested?" Jolene said with indignant rage.

"I don't know," Heck told her. "White men's laws and Indian's laws aren't the same thing. It'd be your word against his. Unless Rufus Buck would turn on him, and I doubt he'd ever do that, even to save his own skin."

Jolene stared at him in angry dismay, then went back to Ellie's side and held her hand as the Cherokee chanting lapsed to silence.

As if in unintended counterpoint to the tribal chant, Captain Edmund read from Ecclesiastes 1: 8 which he knew to be one of Judge Parker's favorite passages:

"To everything there is a season, and a time to every purpose under heaven. A time to be born, a time to die.

A time to plant and a time to pluck up that which is planted. A time to kill and a time to kill. A time to break down, and a time to build up. A time to weep, and a time to laugh. A time to mourn, and a time to dance. A time to cast away stones, and a time to gather stones together. A time to embrace, and a time to refrain from embracing. A time to gain, and a time to lose. A time to keep, and a time to cast away. A time to rend, and a time to sew. A time to love, and a time to hate. A time of war, and a time of peace."

Having come to the end of the psalm, he said, "Ashes to ashes, dust to dust, and may eternal life shine upon him. Amen."

Then Ellie wiped her eyes, stifled her tears and spoke firmly. "I loved my husband dearly, and he died trying to protect me. We were alone together, trying to carry on after we lost my father and his brother in the Civil War. My dear Spencer will always remain in my heart until we meet again in heaven. But I want to thank all of you for the help you've given me and for all that you have done today, out of the goodness of your hearts. I believe that no particular race has a monopoly on goodness of the heart. And all of you have once again shown me the simple truth of that belief. God bless each and every one of you. And may peace and happiness be yours from this time forward."

27

A t the Fort Smith Jail, Seth Crosby was sitting on a bentwood chair in front of the cells where Rufus Buck and his followers were being held. With his pencil and notebook ready, he dearly wanted the big scoop of getting an interview with the gang, especially Rufus himself, and he scoured his mind for some incentive that he might offer them. He knew they had but little contact with the outside world, so he supposed that they might want more information from him than he wanted from them. This was because their court-appointed lawyer had made just one of two cursory trips here. He wasn't very actively doing his job but was merely going through the motions, and nobody was trying to hold his feet to the coals, not even the prisoners, it seemed, because even they knew it was a foregone conclusion that they would all be hanged.

Crosby wasn't fool enough to try to persuade them otherwise. He knew he'd only gain cooperation from them if they thought he had something to offer. All the while he was glad that the bars kept them back from him a few feet, because even at that distance he could barely stand the smell. Giving prisoners an opportunity to bathe wasn't a priority for the jailers. George Maledon once joked that God would send them to hell even if they repented, just to get rid of the smell.

Seth Crosby said, "From what I hear, you guys don't have anything going for you as a defense, so this is your chance to tell your side of the story."

Lukey sneeringly said, "You sayin' we're not gonna get a chance to testify?

"You're entitled to that, but the prosecutor will be licking his lips to get you on the stand. Believe me, he'll tear you to shreds. So your counsel will advise you to throw yourselves on the mercy of the court."

Rufus said, "Ha! *What* fuckin' mercy? Parker is the Hangin' Judge! And he loves the title and wants to hang onto it."

Crosby ventured to say, "Maybe you should have thought of that before you chose a life of crime."

He knew when he said it that it wasn't going to endear him to his coveted interviewees, but he couldn't help himself. Secretly he found them contemptible.

"You sound like a fuckin' fairy," Sam Sampson told him.

"You can insult me all you want," Crosby said, "but I'm out here and you're in there."

Lukey said, "How's about we tell you our story and you sneak us a hacksaw?"

The others cracked up.

Lewis asked, "If we agree to tell you everything you want to know, what do we get out of it?"

Crosby made mental calculations, then said, "I think I can get my editor to pay you in the neighborhood of two hundred, maybe two-hundred and fifty dollars."

"Hmph!" Lukey scoffed. "Where we gonna spend it when our necks are stretched?"

His cellmates guffawed.

Crosby said, "Don't you want to buy better treatment while you're in here? Better food? You've got the trial to go through, and that's not till next week or the week after. And it'll likely take at least two weeks. Then, if you lose, which you're probably going to, you still have the appeals process. So it'd be really nice to have a couple hundred dollars in your kick to buy yourselves better food now and then, or nicer clothes to put on when you go in front of the jury."

"Don't shit me!" Rufus barked. "They ain't gonna let us buy nicer clothes! They're gonna drag us into that courtroom in shackles and we'll still stink to high heaven like we do now! The jury won't deliberate long just 'cause they don't wanna smell us anymore!"

Crosby thought that Rufus Buck had just made a valid and sort of comical point, but he didn't want to say so and didn't want to venture a smile. So he scrambled for a good angle to push and finally said, "Well, you want to be as famous as possible, don't you? *Frank Leslie's Illustrated Newspaper* will make that happen. Jesse James was actually just a stone cold killer, but we cleaned up his image and now people worship him as if he was a Confederate hero who was deeply wronged."

"We probably killed more people than Jesse did," Rufus Buck said. "Not that he killed in the war, but afterwards."

Seth Crosby knew that most of the ones that Jesse killed in the war, as one of Quantrill's Raiders, were just innocent Yankee civilians. But he didn't say so.

28

Tommy and Jolene Palmer were sitting at a picnic table in a small city park when George Maledon sat down with them and handed them each a bottle of soda. It was a Sunday, the drugstore wasn't open today, and Tommy had sneaked out of the house past his grandma without wearing what he thought of as his "sissy suit" of a shirt, tie and knickers. Jolene was wearing jeans and a crisply creased pink short-sleeved blouse that she had pressed herself using a heavy iron heated over coals in her grandma's fireplace. Her hair was let loose down to her shoulders, and George didn't doubt that she must think it to be more "grown-up" than her usual pigtails.

Tommy smiled a little, but Jolene didn't, when they thanked him for the sodas. He could tell she was upset about something and thought it might be about seeing Peta Nocona at Spencer Patterson's burial and learning that he was the one who had been itching to buy her.

George said, "You know I care about you kids. I feel really bad about what you both went through."

"Am I gonna get to testify at the trial?" Jolene asked after sipping her soda.

"No, I'm afraid not," George said. "Would you have wanted to?"

Letting go with the full force of her anger, Jolene said, "Yes, I *do* want to! I want to help them get *hanged!*"

"I understand," George said, hoping to dissuade her. "But the prosecutor's idea is that he wants to hold you two in reserve, and it's a wise strategy in my opinion. If something happens and he doesn't get the guilty verdict he's after, then he can charge them all over again for the murders of your family members."

Tommy pursed his lips sadly. George thought that sometimes he looked even younger than ten, with his smooth, unblemished face, blue eyes and blond hair. But like many boys he could barely wait to be a grown-up, and he would have resented hearing himself being described boyishly. By the same token, George felt a fatherly fondness toward him but didn't know how to express it without making him uncomfortable.

"That Rufus Buck bunch did so much bad stuff," he said. "Who would ever vote them innocent?"

"Well, defendants aren't voted innocent, it's either guilty or not guilty, and it's meant to be beyond a reasonable doubt. So they can be guilty, and everyone knows their guilty, but the jury doesn't feel it's been totally proven. So prosecutors don't like to take chances. By holding back on your testimony, he might get two swings at the ball."

Tommy pleaded, "Can you talk to him, or to the judge? They might listen to you. Beg them to let us testify. Will you?"

"I can try to get them to revisit the subject," George promised.

"What about that horrible old Indian who wanted to buy me and make me sleep with him?" Jolene said with increased anger. "He shouldn't be able to get away with that. What's going to happen to him?"

"There are federal laws against what's called bigamy," George said. "Mostly they got passed by Congress to clamp down on Brigham Young and his congregation in Utah. But the Indian tribes legally have their own laws and their own courts, and sometimes our regular government either doesn't have full jurisdiction or the jurisdiction issue is shaky."

"You mean that damned Indian can get away with it!" Jolene snapped as she pushed hard against the table and stood up, glowering.

"Well, we're supposed to be a nation of laws," George said. "That's what the Founding Fathers believed in. And I've spent a lifetime trying to live up to it."

"By hanging people?" Jolene said snottily. "How does that make you better than anyone else?"

It was a good question, George thought, because it was one that he had wrestled with often in the middle of the night. Especially when he woke up tormented by his sins.

Jolene stormed out of the little park, leaving him and Tommy just sitting there by themselves, and they both watched her go. Then Tommy got up and followed her.

29

After lunch, Seth Crosby finally got the rapists and murderers to consent to an interview and allow him to take notes.

Lukey said, "My daddy was a mean black man with scars that looked like big fat worms tryin' to bust outta his skin. He was a slave on a plantation, and he was given a hundred lashes with a bullwhip for tryin' to run away. He almost had both of his feet chopped off by the overseer. My mama was Creek, and he beat her somethin' awful and he always made me watch. You would think that him bein' a freed slave would make him not wanna use the same kind of brutal shit that was done on him. But instead it was the only way he knew how to treat any other human bein' includin' his own son."

Seth asked, "Do you think that the viciousness you experienced in your childhood caused you to go astray?"

"Well, let's get somethin' straight, Mister goddamned Seth," I never went astray. What I did was I decided to take revenge. When the whites took me away from my people and put me in the Indian School, the white teachers were kind to me on the surface, but I still hated them because I knew that underneath their holy fuckin' faces they were sure they were the chosen ones and I was an Injun piece of shit. I didn't want their charity, I wanted to rob and kill them. I used to stare at the gold plate and goblet on their altar and try to figger out how I could snatch it and get my ass the hell outta there for good."

Seth scribbled in his notebook, then turned to Rufus, who was Lukey's cellmate. "What about you, Rufus? What do you remember from your childhood?"

"My parents were the opposite of Lukey's. My mama was black and my daddy was Creek. Nothin' about them was mean. They loved their simple life with the tribe. When I was real little, that was okay, and I didn't see nothin' wrong with it. But when I learned more about what was done to our people on the Trail of Tears and afterwards, even to this day, I started to hate my mommy and daddy for bein' so meek, and for tryin' to be white. My mommy used to have awful spells that went back to her days in the Indian School when the damn nuns tried to bleach all the Cherokee out of her. I loved my grandpa, and he used to tell me stories about back when the Indians freely roamed the plains and there were millions of buffalo that the Great Spirit created for them. But when I was nine years old and asked what happened to those millions of buffalo, he said the whities killed them all and had a hero who shot the most, and they called him Buffalo Bill. And when the buffalo were gone, the Indians had to die, because there were no buffalo for them to hunt for eating, or for using their hides to make their clothes or their teepees. That's only one reason why I hate the whites."

Seth said, "But you fellows didn't just rape and kill

white people, Rufus. The Creeks and the blacks were your victims as well."

Rufus didn't give that much thought. But he said, "I can't explain it all, and I don't want to. I just came to hate the world and everybody in it for not letting the world be the way the Great Spirit wanted it to be. In the white people's Bible it says that their God drowned them in a flood for bein' so evil and sinful. Well then, why did He let them live again and take the land from us Indians? Why couldn't He see that they still needed to be punished and destroyed? So I wanted to do it to help the Great Spirit."

Seth Crosby lapsed into thoughtfulness for a while, then put away his pencil and notebook. "Well," he said, "this has all been very enlightening, and I think it will gain you some degree of sympathy among my readers. I hope you will enlighten me further when I come back tomorrow. Goodbye for now, fellows."

He got up, put his bowler hat on, and departed.

As soon as they heard the jailhouse door slam, the gang burst into howls of laughter, slapping their thighs and collapsing onto their bunks with hilarity.

"He ate it up hook, line and sinker!" Lukey exclaimed.

Rufus said, "What a great line of bullshit you came up with, Lukey! You oughtta be the writer, not him!"

Sam said, "Do either of you really give a shit about the buffalo or the Great Spirit?"

"Hell, no!" Rufus told him. "I might have, if I'd lived back then—but I wouldn't know a buffalo from a bull moose! The whites had 'em all kilt way before I was born! I don't even think there *is* a goddamn Great Spirit, but that faggoty reporter believes any kinda bullshit we wanna feed him!"

30

Blanton Hughes, the blustery man wearing green suspenders and a green bowler hat who had led the near-lynching of the Rufus Buck gang in Muskogee, got all fired up again over Seth Crosby's freshly published article in *Frank Leslie's Illustrated Newspaper*, with a blaring black headline:

THE RUFUS BUCK GANG! MURDERERS, RAPISTS & WHITE SLAVERS!

The only known photograph of the gang was splashed on the front page, and it grabbed Blanton Hughes's attention as he was about to stagger past the newsstand, drunk as usual. He dug into a front pocket of his baggy brown corduroy trousers and came up with a quarter to buy the newspaper. Then he sat at a lunch counter and sobered himself up somewhat by downing several large cups of black coffee while he read the article over and over growing more and more angry and self-righteous and hateful.

"Shoulda lynched 'em last week when we had the chance," he muttered to himself, and in a fit of rage he banged the counter and splashed coffee on his rumpled white shirt, which already was stained and smelled of puke from last night's binge. This made him angrier, and he smacked his forehead with the palm of his hand.

He had joined the Arkansas Ku Klux Klan when he was only seventeen, and had gotten praised by the Grand Wizard for devising a "practical joke" that he worked over and over on ex-slaves. Wearing a hideously ghoulish mask and a bullet-riddled Confederate tunic, he'd show up at a farm that was being worked by black shareholders. He'd moan piteously till someone dared to peek out, then he'd feign an eerie, ghost-like voice and demand water from the well bucket. He would drink several buckets full, not letting the sharecropper see that the water was being diverted into a concealed rubber tube, and all the while he'd be moaning that he hadn't had a thing to drink since he was killed on the battlefield at Shiloh. Then he'd gallop off into the night, and blacks for miles around would come to believe that the Confederate dead were haunting the countryside. It was often enough to scare them into fleeing. And Klan members thought of it as harmless mischief because they didn't have to kill anybody.

But Blanton Hughes didn't have anything against lynching when he thought it was well deserved. As in the case of the Rufus Buck gang. But he regretted that he hadn't had the luck to carry it out.

Now his sensibilities were being assaulted by the fresh information that they had tried to sell a fourteen-year-old girl into sexual slavery. And the buyer lived close by. He was a Cherokee named Peta Nocona and his lodge was in Dog Town.

Good. An easy target. But don't get over-confident, he told himself.

The crowd that had swarmed the Muskogee Jail when the Buck gang was first brought there wasn't a creature of planning. It had come together of its own volition, and all Blanton had to do was talk loudly and boldly enough to become one of its leaders. That self-congregating kind of thing wasn't going to happen this time. But he figured he didn't need a mob because he didn't need to storm a jail guarded by lawmen. Eight tough, bold and strongly motivated hombres with a thirst for justice would be enough.

He recruited them from his Ku Klux enclave and they rode out on a starlit Thursday night, eight on horseback, including the leader, Blanton Hughes, and a ninth man driving a buckboard with an eight-foot cross and a big can of kerosene in the bed of the wagon. The cross was made of two-by-fours nailed together in the middle, with rags wrapped around the wood and wound with cord. The end that would be driven into the ground had already been sharpened with an axe. There was a box of canning jars in the wagon, padded with rags so they wouldn't clink. The jars were already filled with kerosene and had cloth wicks inserted, ready to be lit.

Blanton Hughes was sure that thorough preparation, excellent planning and perfect timing would be the key to getting the mission accomplished and not getting caught. He and his fellow Ku Kluxers rode through the night without speaking till they got within range of their objective, then they tethered their horses and parked the buckboard a mile down the road from Peta Nocona's property.

They put on their white sheets and hoods, not because they intended to show themselves and make a

Klan-type ruckus by dancing and shouting around a fiery cross, but because just in case something went wrong, they didn't want to be recognized. Feeling sly, bold and powerful, they walked in near silence the rest of the way to Nocona's stucco house. Two of them had been assigned to carry the cross, two to carry the box of jars, and two to carry the can of kerosene.

The plan was to jam the sharpened cross into wherever there was soft earth, get it lit, and then light the kerosene bombs and toss them into the house, causing a conflagration. Also, they knew there were three teepees, and they would each get hit by a flaming bottle. Anyone who rushed out of the house or the teepees would be gunned down. Anyone who survived wounds or burns would be hanged. And the cross would be left blazing to inspire terror and fear of the Klan as they ran back to the wagon and the horses and galloped away, just like Blanton used to do when he was impersonating a Confederate ghost.

Things started to go wrong because a rather simple glitch: the ground was too hard. The jammed the sharpened end of the cross into the packed ground and it didn't go in far enough to stand it up. Two of them got on each side of the crossbar and pulled all at once as hard as they could, trying to ram it in.

"A rock," one of them whispered. "We're hittin' a goddamn rock!"

"Shhh!" one of his buddies cautioned.

It was hard for them to hear each other with their hoods on.

All four of the guys who had hold of the crossbeam lifted it aloft once again and rammed in unison as hard as they could into what they hoped was soft enough earth to get it in deep.

To their silent joy, the cross seemed to stand up well enough. So they struck a match and set the whole works afire.

The fiery blaze lit up the night. And it also lit *them* up —which made them excellent targets for the lookouts that Petra Nocona had posted around his property, in the surrounding woods and up on a hill. Peta had hired them because they were such excellent shots with their Winchesters. He thought he needed them after his private business came out, starkly exposed for all to see, in the slanderous article that appeared in *Frank Leslie's Illustrated Newspaper*.

The posted security guards instantly blasted away at the four intruders who had planted the burning cross. In their white sheets and hoods they stood out so clearly in the light of the blazing flames that they were all hit with kill shots and fell down dead.

Two others were advancing toward the stucco house wielding kerosene jars with lit fuses, and they both went down with severe chest and stomach wounds. Another rapid volley finished them off.

The other two were running toward the teepees with more fire bombs, and their legs were shot out from under them. They writhed on the ground in screaming agony until they were put out of their misery with head shots.

That left only one of the nine who had come here uninvited: Blanton Hughes. He hid behind one of the buckboard's iron wheels and tried frantically to get at his pistol, but it got tangled up in his sheet.

Peta Nocona came out of his stucco house and shot Blanton in his arm, causing his pistol to drop out from under his sheet.

The burning cross fell over but continued to burn.

"Thank you for giving my men well-lighted targets," Peta said.

Blanton moaned and cried, and started pleading for his life. His moans and cries were somewhat muffled by his white hood until Peta Nocona pulled it off and threw it onto the ground.

"What a silly costume," Peta said.

His three squaws came out of their teepee and fetched pails of water from their well to extinguish what was left of the cross on the ground.

Blanton continued to beg and cry.

Peta said, "First you and I will talk, and you will be made to tell me all you know. Then we will find out how you will enjoy being skinned alive."

31

———

Judge Isaac Parker had a deep, respectful admiration for the new federal courthouse for the Western District of Arkansas. A monumental three-story brick building of many windows, for air and light, it was built in 1890 and also housed a main branch of the United States Post Office. The cannon in the front of it was a monument in and of itself, as it had been used at Fort Pitt during a furious battle of the Civil War.

The judge's office was only a half mile away from the courthouse, and he preferred to walk it. Both buildings were on Sixth Street in this town of eleven thousand people on the banks of the Arkansas River. The main street, Garrison Avenue, was of unpaved hard-packed dirt, but impressively wide, with room for carriages four abreast. It boasted sidewalks with gas lighting and streetcars.

Judge Parker liked to detour past Garrison on his way to Sixth, so he could pass by the beautiful modern opera house. He had worked hard to help tame this town ever since he was appointed to the bench almost sixteen years ago, and he took great satisfaction in its modernity. He liked walking past the thriving establishments such shops and restaurants, but also the factories. Two of his favorite places were the Mowen & Johnson Dry Goods store, where his wife liked to look at some of the fine women's apparel that they could not afford, and the Union Furniture Company, one of the South's leading manufacturers of not just regular household furniture but also pieces that were acquired by the wealthy for their mansions.

He considered it his sworn duty not to allow rapists and murderers to destroy what decent citizens had wrought. To that end, he used a governmentally financed force of over two hundred marshals, and up till now sixty-five of them had been killed in the line of duty. One murderous outlaw had said to the marshal who arrested him, "Don't take me before Parker, you might as well kill me now." True enough, he had sentenced one hundred and sixty men to hang, but often people did not realize that due to appeals and commutations only seventy-nine of them had actually met the gallows. He said, "It wasn't I who hanged them. I never hung a man. It was the law." In many cases he had no choice because the Statutes of the United States commanded that "anyone convicted of murder or rape shall suffer death."

Judge Parker always strove to be fair, impartial and hard-working. He kept his court in session six days a week, twelve hours per day. As each case began, he admonished the jurors, "Permit no innocent man to be punished but let no guilty man escape justice."

The trial of the Rufus Buck gang was to begin today, and when his morning walk took him closer to the court-house, the crowd grew thicker and thicker. But he was held in so much awe and was so highly feared and respected that people readily moved aside for him without having to be admonished or shoved out of the way by the uniformed policemen guarding the front doors.

At eight o'clock sharp, in his black robe he made his entrance and sat pontifically behind the highly polished and elevated oaken bench. The courtroom was already packed with people so excited they could hardly sit still. Gawkers in the gallery leaned forward in case the judge was going to say something, but he ignored them by fiddling with his notes. He had seen that Heck Thomas and George Maledon were in the third row, behind the attorneys' table, which for now remained empty because the defendants had not yet been brought in.

He felt that this brand new courtroom was more appropriate venue for the majesty of the law than was the former courtroom that had become too small and shabby. Under the gaslight chandeliers, a newfangled commodity, there were twelve jurors' chairs, a witness chair and two attorney tables. Behind the bar there were three dozen spectator seats, with gleaming brass spittoons placed at intervals. There were no spittoons in front of the bar where their use might mar the red carpet. The spectators' area was uncarpeted but was tiled for easy cleanup.

When the prosecutors came in and took seats at their table, the murmurs of the crowd picked up in intensity. Seth Crosby perked up also. He and the other reporters were seated among the spectators.

The throng froze into rapt attention when Judge Parker rapped his gavel and ordered the defendants to be brought in.

They were in chains, accompanied by their attorney. They emerged from a side door—Rufus Buck, Sam Sampson, Lewis Davis and Lukey Davis—gawking around sheepishly, except for Rufus, who showed everybody his middle finger, holding it up and waving it around as if in their faces.

There were only three women in the crowd, and they gasped, fanned themselves and averted their eyes from Rufus's obscene gesture.

Three big, heavily bearded men in bibbed coveralls and scuffed boots jumped up in an overpowering urge to pummel the chained-up criminals, but unformed bailiffs grabbed them and used harsh threats to get them seated again, threatening to evict them if they couldn't control themselves.

Two other bailiffs slammed Rufus down onto a chair a little behind the defense table, but the other three prisoners were allowed to sit down without being manhandled.

Judge Parker pounded his gavel and the nearest bailiff to him shouted, "Order in the court!" until he obtained sufficient silence.

Then the jury, twelve men and no women, were ushered in amidst the unrelenting stares and murmurs of the courtroom crowd.

When all were seated and quieted down again, the judge spoke in somber tones.

"Each of the accused has entered a plea of Not Guilty. Accordingly, I must remind the jury that it is their legal right to claim innocence, and they are not to be prejudged, no matter how much hearsay, rumor and gossip may have accrued to them. They are presumed to be innocent under the law until proven otherwise. Therefore I must remind you that, as loyal and thoughtful citizens, you must permit no innocent man to be punished and let no guilty man escape. With that in mind, is the prosecution ready to call their first witness?"

One of the attorneys, a bald, red-faced man in a gray suit and vest, arose and faced the jury. "Good morning, Judge Parker and ladies and gentlemen of the jury. I am Jefferson Irving, the lead prosecutor, and I summon Mrs. Rosetta Hansen to take the stand."

All eyes fastened on a rear door where they knew that all witnesses were to be escorted into the courtroom by bailiffs.

The chained-up defendants turned in their seats to sneer at the first witness against them.

Rosetta Hansen was a comely, well-dressed woman about thirty years old, wearing a nice yellow dress and a flowery bonnet, and she proceeded slowly but resolutely to the witness stand.

The head bailiff handed her a Bible, and she placed her right hand upon it>

"Do you swear by Almighty God to tell the truth, the whole truth and nothing but the truth?"

"I do," she answered.

And Judge Parker said, "You may please take the stand."

Prosecutor Irving said, "Can you recognize and point out the men you accused of assaulting you?"

She pointed at the defendants.

Mr. Irving said, "Let the record show that Mrs. Hansen has identified the four defendants in this case. Now, then, Rosetta, I would like you to just tell the jury, in your own words, in as much detail as you might recall, what these defendants did to you on August fifth, 1995."

Rosetta took a long moment to pull herself together for her ordeal. But once she was ready, she spoke clearly and with conviction, often trembling and failing to control her tears.

"It was on a Monday, the worst day of my life. I was hanging out the wash and my husband, Henry, was sleeping in a hammock under our grape arbor, when this horrid gang rode through our front gate. Henry woke up, hearing the hoof beats, and asked them if they were hunters because of seeing their weapons. They just laughed and asked for water, so Henry sent my little brother down to the stream to fetch a pail. Then one of them doffed his hat, and that's when my husband and I both recognized Lewis Davis, who we had caught trying to steal some tools from us just a couple of months before, but he pleaded with us not to press charges, but to give him a chance."

This brought murmurs, fidgets and disparaging glances at the defendants from the jury and the onlookers.

Judge Parker picked up his gavel and this time it was enough to quiet them.

He said, "Go on, please, Mrs. Hansen, you have our rapt attention."

"When we recognized Lewis Davis, we knew we were at the mercy of brigands because by this time everybody on the remote farms and ranches had heard about the Rufus Buck gang and who was in it. We knew they were going around raping and murdering. So my husband started for a corner of the house, hoping against hope he wouldn't arouse their suspicions and would be able to lay his hands on his Winchester. He gained the corner safely, then ran for the door, but was stopped by Lukey Davis, who had rushed in from the front of the house and got to the Winchester before my husband could. He just laughed and shoved the muzzle into Henry's stomach and forced him back out into the yard, where Rufus Buck said with an ugly sneer, 'I'm Cherokee Bill's brother and we want all your money, so you better give it up!' Well, we knew that Cherokee Bill had been hanged, and deservedly so, and it might be true that he had a brother who was every bit as evil. But true or not that they were related, it didn't matter to us because we knew for certain that we would be lucky if we lived to see another day on this earth."

At this, Defense Attorney William Cravens jumped to his feet.

"Objection! Mrs. Hansen's reference to Cherokee Bill is prejudicial! Totally without any corroboration, it connects my clients to a known criminal who was executed! Thus, it conflicts with their presumption of innocence!"

Craven's protest drew a chorus of boos from the onlookers—and Judge Parker pounded his gavel. "We must have complete order in my court!" he said quite sternly. "Any further outbursts will be met with expulsion—and with a heavy monetary penalty."

Things quieted down pretty quickly. Heck Thomas and George Maledon cast looks at each other signifying that they both knew this was the judge being the judge.

"The objection is denied," Judge Parker then said. "You may go on, Mrs. Hansen. Do you need a handkerchief? A glass of water?"

She nodded, and the head bailiff stepped forward to hand her the water and a big red men's bandana, which brought forth a couple of titters.

She made use of both, however, and then continued. "Rufus Buck leveled a string of vile curses at my husband for trying to get to his rifle, and he kept shoving the weapon in Henry's face and saying he was going to pull the trigger. Then Lukey Davis said they would kill Henry if I didn't do what they wanted, which was to ravage me, each of them, one right after another, after drawing poker cards to determine who would go first. I begged them not to hurt my little children, a boy and a girl, both toddlers, in their cribs for their afternoon nap, and Lukey said, 'If you don't willingly let us have you, we'll throw the damn brats into the river.' And I knew they'd actually do it."

There were gasps and murmured curses from some of the onlookers, but most of the jury members managed to retain their composure.

Mrs. Hansen said, "They said they would kill Henry if I didn't do everything they wanted, and they took me behind the barn and made me undress, and then they... they brutally ravaged me."

She broke into tears, her whole body shaking uncontrollably. For a long while, she couldn't manage to pull herself together while everybody in the packed courtroom looked on, totally appalled and in complete sympathy with the aggrieved witness—except for the accused men, who smiled and smirked at one another as if they were choosing to not give a damn about the nails she was driving into their coffin.

To urge her to calm herself a bit more, Judge Parker spoke to her softly, with kindness in his voice. "Just go on as best you can, Mrs. Hansen, and tell us all that you endured. I'm afraid that the law makes it necessary for you to tell it. It is a very delicate matter, of course, but you will have to tell about what more they did, if you are able."

Prosecutor Irving addressed her once again. "Mrs. Hansen, are you saying that only one of the brutes did this to you? Or did all four do it?"

"At the time of the assault, there were five of them, not four. But I understand that one of them, named Maoma July, was killed during an atrocity upon yet another family."

Once again Counselor Cravens jumped to his feet, saying, "I object! Any purported assault on another family is not in evidence!"

"But soon will be," said Irving.

Judge Parker thought about it, then said, "For the time being I'm going to allow the objection."

"But, Your Honor—"

"No, I'm going to allow it, Mr. Irving. Your line of inquiry can come back in, once you've established its relationship to Mrs. Hansen's testimony. Go ahead, Mr. Irving. proceed with your questions to her."

"Rosetta," Irving said, "tell us why you submitted to the vicious indignities that you have described. Why did you not just accept your own death by defying them, as the saints in the Holy Bible are said to have done?"

Rosetta broke into uncontrollable tears again. Then she wiped her eyes with the bandana, took a small sip of water, and continued.

"I wanted desperately to save my husband and my babies. I told myself that if I could prevent the rest of my family from being killed, my own life wouldn't matter. But, God help me, I think a part of me wished to save my own life as well. And now I am living the wretched existence that I probably deserve, because I didn't have the courage of the saints and martyrs that I believe in."

Upon hearing those words from her, most of the men, let alone the few women in the courtroom, were having to wipe tears from their cheeks.

Even Judge Parker, who was trying to remain stoically aloof for the sake of not prejudicing the jury, was obliged to remove his eyeglasses and brush his fingers across his eyelids before finding the right words to speak, sympathetically.

"Rosetta, it is apparent to me that you are a young wife and mother of supreme courage and an abiding love of your husband and your children. You have committed no sin in the eyes of a merciful Almighty God. Your conscience is blameless, your soul is without blemish in this matter. And your contribution to the sanctity of this court and the justice I am sworn to uphold is unassailable. I hope you can go forth from this day forward and enjoy the pious life that you and your Christian family so richly deserve."

A murmur of assent and approbation came from the people.

With tears still streaming down her cheeks, Rosetta spoke her final words for her day in the courtroom.

"Thank you, Judge Parker. And thanks to all of you who have stood by me and have forgiven me for my misfortune."

Judge Parker sadly shook his head over all that had transpired.

He announced, "There will now be a one-hour adjournment for lunch. The jury will report back here to resume duty at two o'clock."

He rapped his gavel three times, then arose to disrobe, thankful he'd get out from under the heat and the perspiration under his robe.

32

As the court was adjourning, Jolene and Tommy waited in the little town park, hoping that George Maledon would show up, as promised.

Jolene didn't feel as confident as her little brother did. She asked him, "Is Mr. Maledon coming for sure? He said, soon as the court went into recess. And it seemed like that was an hour ago, when we watched the jurors file out."

Tommy said, "I don't think it's been an hour yet. More like a half hour. And he always keeps his word."

Just then, George came strolling into the park, approaching the two kids. He wasn't wearing his usual grim black suit and he carried no weapons. For today he had dressed in his only other suit, a plain brown one, with a red tie that was, for him, the height of flamboyancy.

"You look nice," Jolene said.

He sat across from them at the picnic bench and gave them a tentative smile. "I'd have been here sooner," he explained, "but Judge Parker is a tough cookie. I had to argue my tail off in chambers, but he and the lead prose-cutor finally said they'd let Jolene testify."

Frowning, Tommy said, "What about *me?*"

"Sorry, I didn't agree with them but they maintained that you're too young, and even if it ain't true, which I know it's not, the defense counsel would be able to persuade the jury that you'd have been easily coached."

"But is isn't true at all!" Tommy blurted, near to tears. "I saw them kill my dad! And I saw what they did to my mom!"

"I'm sorry, but their point was that you didn't actu-ally witness it when it was happening, you just saw things that had already happened. The judge believes you, Tommy. But he's worried that someone on the jury might not, and that might cause a mistrial. You want them to be convicted and punished, don't you?"

"I'd hang them myself if I could!" Tommy said vehemently.

George believed that this wasn't the mere rebellion of a ten-year-old but was the same kind of railing against society's injustices that was indulged in by many adults.

Jolene asked him, "What about that old Indian, Peta Nocona, or whatever his name is? Is anything gonna happen to him? I think he ought to be shot."

"Funny you should say that, because somebody tried to do just that," George said without any sadness over it. "We heard about it but we have no proof it actually happened. Supposedly the Ku Klux Klan came and burned a cross in front of his house, and they were gonna burn the house down, too, and probably string him up."

"Why would they do that?" Jolene asked. "He's not black, is he? I thought the Klan only goes after black people."

"Lots of them hate anybody who ain't white," George told her. "Especially if they sleep with white women. And he has a couple of white squaws, I think you already know that."

"I wish they'd slit his throat while he's asleep!" Jolene blurted with intense feeling.

"Well, we don't know who tried to burn him out and we'll probably never find out," George said. "He has a tendency to just take care of his own problems and keep his mouth shut about it."

"I read Seth Crosby's article about the Rufus Buck gang in *Frank Leslie's Illustrated Newspaper*. It's on the newsstand at my grandparents' drugstore, and I sneaked peeks at it while they weren't lookin'. He wrote about how that Indian wanted to buy a white girl, but he never told it was Jolene."

"Thank God!" Jolene said, and she crossed herself.

"Crosby is really not a bad guy," George said. "He has some decency in him, and he didn't want you to get the wrong kind of attention."

"I wish I could be at the trial," Tommy said. "Are they for sure gonna be hanged, George?"

"Looks like a foregone conclusion," George said. "Your sister will help make it happen. She's on the docket for first thing tomorrow morning."

This sudden revelation hit Jolene and Tommy like a thunderbolt.

"For *real?*" Jolene exclaimed, totally excited.

"Does a bear poop in the woods?" George asked her.

"I feel left out," Tommy said morosely.

"What about Ellie Patterson?" Jolene asked keenly. "*She* has a lot to tell. Right?"

"She'll be on the witness stand this afternoon,"

George said. "Between the two of you, Rufus and his bunch of cretins won't stand a chance."

"Darn it! *I* want a chance!" Tommy said petulantly.

"Think of it this way," George told him. "Your sister is acting on your behalf."

"Just because I'm only ten!" Tommy blurted. "It's not fair! I wanna testify about my daddy! I was the one who was with him when they killed him. Not Jolene or anybody else."

33

The jury took their seats and Judge Parker rapped his gavel for silence at eight o'clock in the morning on the second day of the trial.

He said, "This court is now in session. Mr. Irving, is the prosecution ready with another witness?"

"Yes, Your Honor. The prosecution now calls Jolene Palmer. She is only fourteen years old, but she's a bright young lady, quite mature for her age. Her testimony is germane, and she has the intelligence and comportment to deliver it." His confidence was genuine because he had interviewed her and coached where appropriate, yesterday evening.

"All right," said Judge Parker. "The bailiff will escort Miss Palmer into our presence."

All eyes turned toward her as she made her entrance and proceeded toward the witness stand. She was wearing her hair in childlike pigtails again, and her prim, proper white blouse and blue jumper was not in any way adult-like. This was the image she had been coached to project by one of the assistants to the lead prosecutor.

As she took her oath to tell the truth and nothing but the truth, she looked toward Ellie Patterson, who was seated at the prosecution table. The older woman flashed Jolene a reassuring smile conveying that she if she had gotten through it, so could Jolene. Her being there was yet another strategy promulgated by the lead prosecutor. She was dressed as simply as Jolene was, basically the same as when she had testified, with no jewelry.

Judge Parker said, "The witness may be seated."

And when Jolene sat in the witness chair, she looked small and vulnerable.

Prosecutor Irving said, "State your name, please, honey."

Defense attorney Cravens immediately jumped to his feet.

"Objection! The prosecutor should refrain from using endearing words with this witness in an obvious attempt to curry sympathy."

Several onlookers booed, and Judge Parker rapped his gavel.

Mr. Irving said, with some amusement, "I shall henceforth refrain from endearing nouns and adjectives, Your Honor."

This brought titters from the crowd and almost from a couple members of the jury. But the judge maintained a rigidly sober demeanor and said, "Very well, sir. You may proceed with your questioning."

Irving said, "State your name and age, please, Miss Palmer."

"Jolene Palmer. I'm fourteen."

"You have previously come forward with an account of certain crimes committed against you and your family members. Do you see any of the persons you accuse of those crimes in this courtroom?"

"There they are! Those four men, right over there!"

She pointed with great anger at the four defendants.

"Do you know their names by any chance?"

"I can never forget them, because of what they did. Rufus Buck, Sam Sampson, and Lewis and Lukey Davis."

"Was there a fifth perpetrator?"

"Yes, but I killed him. That's how I almost got away."

Gasps and murmurs went up when she admitted to killing someone.

Irving let it sink in for a while. Then he asked, "What did these men do? Why were you trying to get away from them? Can you tell it in your own words to this jury?"

Jolene pursed her lips with anger and inner resolve. She said, "I want to tell it. I begged to come here and tell it, even though people said I'm too young. Thank you, Judge Parker, for letting me be here."

"Thank *you*, young lady. I applaud your courage."

Mr. Cravens cut in, saying, "You're giving me ample grounds for appeal, Your Honor. You just complimented the witness. Some might say you are even coddling her."

The judge got red-faced with anger, and he spoke in no uncertain terms.

"Some might also say, Mr. Cravens, that you are dangerously close to contempt of court and I am dangerously close to imposing it on you, which would result in a huge fine for you and a cooling off period in a jail cell."

This actually elicited a few muted chuckles and a smattering of muted applause.

Judge Parker ignored it all and said, "Proceed with your witness, Mr. Irving."

Irving gave Jolene a sympathetic look.

"Again, just tell what happened in your own words, Miss Palmer."

Jolene summed up her resolve, launched into her story and told it as forcefully as she could, and as it unfolded she made certain to establish firm eye contact with each member of the jury.

"Rufus led his gang onto our ranch, and he was the one wearing a badge, so at first we weren't too afraid. He said he was a sheriff with the Creek Indian Police. That was a lie, but we didn't know it. My grandma and my mom were going to give them food and water, but when they got into the house, they turned on us. They nailed my grandma and my grandpa to the wall, and they started raping my mother, and they made me watch it all, laughing and saying that now they were actually doing me a favor by teaching me all the ways to have sex. But one of them was so drunk and was laughing so hard—the one called Lukey—that he let go of me a little bit, and I ran. He grabbed me by my hair, and a clump of it got ripped out. I ran to the barn, hoping grandpa's horse might still be in there, instead of out in the pasture somewhere. But the horse wasn't in any of the stalls. And I was scared out of my wits, and I needed a weapon, so I grabbed a pitchfork. And the one they called Maoma was the only one who was coming after me right then, so I guess they thought I couldn't get away no matter how much time they took to chase me down. So I waited and hid in a stall, and when Maoma got close I jumped out right behind him, and when he spun around I shoved the pitchfork at him as hard as I could—and it went in him deep—and he was gurgling and clawing at it, but I wouldn't let him pull it out. I kept pushing it in, till he fell down dead."

The jurors, spectators and reporters were stunned by all this, as were also the attorneys. But the four defendants grinned at each other and at the judge and jury and no doubt would have elbowed each other in their ribs if they weren't in their chains and shackles.

Prosecutor Irving waited a long interval to let Jolene's words sink in. He took out his clean white handkerchief and handed it to Jolene so she could wipe her tears. Then he asked, "Did you think you were going to escape from them at that point, Miss Palmer?"

"I thought I might, and I took off running across the field. But by that time, three of them were on their horses, and they ran me down and captured me."

"Were they intending to hold you for ransom?"

"No, but they didn't rape me either, which is what I expected, and I was scared to death of it. They said they were going to sell me to some old Creek Indian who only liked young virgins. He was going to pay them five thousand dollars, but I got away from them before that could happen. But I wouldn't have gotten away if it wasn't for my friend, Ellie Patterson, who was also running away from them because they killed her husband and were going to gang rape her."

Irving shook his head dolefully, once again letting the full impact of Jolene's testimony sink in.

Then he said, "I have no further questions, your honor."

Judge Parker said, "Very well, sir. Would the defense like to question this witness?"

By this time the courtroom crowd had started mumbling and cursing under their breath, but holding back on their anger as much as they could because of the judge's former warnings. He had to bang his gavel several times to quiet them down.

Cravens said, "The defense has no questions for this witness, Your Honor."

"Is the defense ready to present its side of the case?" Judge Parker asked.

"Your Honor, the defense rests," Cravens said.

This stunned everybody, even the prosecutors. They had expected that there would not be anyone called who would testify that the wrong persons had been accused of the crimes. But in their private discussion of strategies, they had figured that the defense might bring forth character witnesses who could talk about good things that the defendants might have done in their lives, or bring out mitigating factors that had caused them to turn bad. All this in an attempt to curry sympathy. But apparently they felt that there was no sympathy to be curried.

Surely they could not argue that the prosecution had not proved its case beyond a reasonable doubt. The only thing left for them to hope for was the mercy of the court. And that was highly unlikely. They must be throwing in the towel because they didn't have a leg to stand on, and they and their pathetic indigent clients knew it.

"Are both sets of attorneys ready for closing arguments?" Judge Parker asked.

They acknowledged that they were. It was not quite ten o'clock. Jolene's testimony had taken a bit less than two hours.

Mr. Cravens, in his summation, assumed the role of the character witnesses that he did not call. He passionately described the long-suffering travails of the Indian peoples, from the invasions of white people, the diseases they brought to America which decimated the native populations, the broken treaties, the wars of conquest, the Trail of Tears, and so on, up to the childhoods of the defendants spent in poverty and prejudice.

Mr. Irving's speech was an angry, indignant retelling

of the ugly, terrifying tales already told in excruciating detail from Rosetta Hansen, Ellie Patterson and Jolene Palmer.

Nothing more needed to be said by the attorneys, and now it was time for the jury to confer in private. They deliberated for less than a half hour before returning their verdict.

Guilty as charged of kidnapping and multiple rapes and the intent to rape.

Judge Parker ordered the prisoners to stand and face him. Then he said, "The jury has found all of you guilty of the crime of rape. The time has arrived when that verdict and its proper punishment is to be pronounced upon you. Have you anything to say as to why that sentence should not be passed?"

"No, Your Honor," said Mr. Cravens.

Judge Parker said to the prisoners, "It behooves all of you to accept the sentence that the court is about to pronounce, not with bravado and braggadocio before men, which counts for nothing, but with earnest preparation to stand before your Maker, the Great Judge of us all, to answer for the offenses you have committed against His children and His Holy Commandments. That is the duty which every man owes in this life, especially men situated as you are now. Your duty now is to make preparation for death and do your best to obtain forgiveness. We are taught that all men can be forgiven by their Maker by approaching Him with penitence and sorrow for the sins they have committed. You must admit to Him in your prayers that you have not led a correct life here on earth, and much less have you prepared yourselves for the hereafter. Because you have been adjudged guilty of reprehensible crimes against the laws of the

United States, you shall be hanged by your necks until dead, and may God, whose laws you have broken, and before whose heavenly tribunal you must appear, have mercy upon your souls."

34

A rhythmic, insistent drum beat, reminiscent of a funeral dirge, overrode the boisterous noise of the thousands of people gathered in the courtyard of Fort Smith, Arkansas, as a platoon of marching soldiers escorted the Rufus Buck gang, in chains and shackles, to the gallows that awaited them.As always on the day of a hanging, the mood of the people was a mixture of awe, drunkenness, satisfaction, excitement, and even edginess and fear concerning what was about to take place. All those emotions were heightened by the anticipation that four villains were to be hanged today, not just one.

Tommy and Jolene Palmer were in the crowd, having sneaked away from supervision of their grandparents by some pretext or other. They were as keyed up as any of the others, or even more so.

The sergeant of the platoon cried "Halt!" at the bottom of the gallows. Then Heck Thomas and George Maledon prodded the four chain-up young criminals up the steps to where four nooses dangled.

Tommy and Jolene pushed and wriggled their way through the crowd to get closer to the gallows. Some people made way for them, muttering about how "the little girl" was the one who had given testimony at the trial.

Heck Thomas and George Maledon spotted them and didn't know what to do about it, considering that they had to remain decorous, so they waved just slightly with their arms down, so as not to be obvious.

Judge Parker made his entrance into the proceedings, escorted through the boisterous crowd by Marshal Haynes and Captain Edmund. They did not ascend the gallows, but stopped at the foot of it. Then the judge made his statement to the men about to die.

"The offense of which you have been convicted shocks all men who are not brutal. It is an attack upon the honor and chastity of women. It is a violation of the virtue of the female heart, and our laws deem it equal in wickedness to the crime of murder. You have not been convicted of murder, though you were certainly guilty of it many times over. You have been convicted of rape, a crime that leaves no room for sympathy. You are guilty of one of the most brutal, wicked, repulsive and dastardly crimes in the annals of inhuman behavior. May the God whose commandments you have broken have mercy upon your souls!"

With that, Judge Parker pivoted and was escorted by Haynes and Edmund back through the throng.

An ominous drum roll sounded.

George Maledon carefully dropped nooses around the necks of each of the condemned, making sure that the thick neck-breaking knots were properly affixed. Then he stepped back and addressed them.

"Any of you have any last words?"

Lukey shouted, dry-mouthed and hoarse, "Goodbye to my sister, Martha!"

Sam said, "I'm glad I'm being hanged at noon so my body can make the one o'clock train to Muskogee!"

Rufus said, "I wrote a poem and left it in my cell. I hope Seth Crosby will take it to my mother and sister or print it in his newspaper."

Crosby had managed to get in close, and he yelled, "You can count on me, Rufus!"

George Maledon asked, "Anything more you boys wanna say?"

None of them piped up, so he put the black hoods over their heads.

He was about to pull the lever, sending them to their doom, when his eyes fell on Tommy Palmer down there, looking upward.

His and Tommy's eyes met.

George thought for a moment, then he motioned Tommy to come up the steps. Two soldiers barred the way so he couldn't pass but George said to them, "These evil bastards lynched this boy's daddy! Let him come on up here!"

The guards looked doubtful, but they let Tommy pass.

Tommy ascended to the gallows, and George took his small hand and placed it under his on the lever. Then he pulled it, or they both did, and the trapdoor sprung, dropping the four murderers to their deaths. Their limp bodies swung and dangled underneath, and the crowd cheered vociferously as George and Tommy stood on the platform and George put his hand on the boy's shoulder.

35

Alone in the jail, Seth Crosby tried the door to Rufus's cell and found that it was unlocked. It swung open with a screeching of its hinges.

With some hesitation, he entered it and looked around.

He spied a wrinkled, dirty piece of paper on the floor and plucked it up, hoping it would be the poem Rufus had written, because it might be worthy of publication. He fully intended to write a follow-up article about the mass execution.

The poem was in Rufus's messy, badly scrawled handwriting, and Seth could barely wait to read it, so he did so without even stepping out of the cell. The title was in the middle of the page, and below it was the poem, barely legible, and with capital letters strewn in lots of places where they didn't belong, even in the middles of words, many of them grossly misspelled.

MY DREAM

I dreAmt I was in HeavEn Among the angels fair I'd neAr
seen, none, so HAndsome THAT twine in golden Hair.
THey looked so Neat and SAng so sweet AND playyed
the Golden HArp.
i WAS about to pick an ANgel ouT and TAke her to my
HEART BUt the momenT i begAn to PleA I thought of
YOU my Love THere wAs none i'D seen so BeAuTiful on
eArTH or HeAven ABove.
GooD, By, My, Dear, MothER and all.so My. Sisters.
RUFUS, BUCK
Youse. Truly

Seth took the note with him to the small park where
George Maledon had mentioned that he was going to be
that afternoon, with Tommy and Jolene.

He sat with the three of them and said, "This is the
poem Rufus Buck left in his cell, written in his own
hand. I'm going to publish it in *Frank Leslie's illustrated
Newspaper*."

He handed it to Tommy, and Jolene peered over her
brother's shoulder while they both read it. Then they
handed it to George.

Tommy said, "I can write a lot better than that." And
he grimaced distastefully at the piece of dirty paper as he
wiped his fingers on his pants.

Jolene said, "So can I. The spelling is atrocious."

Seth said, "Well, you two are very bright, and Rufus
wasn't."

George handed the poem back to Seth and said, "Tell
you the truth, I can't make heads nor tails out of it. And I
can't make no sense outta what that gang done neither."

Seth said, "Well, that's *my* job, George. I'll make it
sound like they were fighting for their land and their

people. Noble savages. My readers will eat it up, believe me."

"My God! That's awful!" Jolene said indignantly.

"Hey, young lady, I've got to make a living," Seth said in his own defense.

George Maledon said, "We'll be in for some big trouble if *all* the Injuns start believin' that crap. What're you tryin' to do, Seth? Get me and Heck killed?"

A LOOK AT: THE DARKEST WEB

John A. Russo, co-writer of the movie *Night of the Living Dead*, spins a tale of greed, corruption, and maliciously evil intent where anyone can become a victim…for the right price…

When Anthropology Professor Neville Pinnock, whose friend and mentor was murdered five years ago, teams up with Fiona Evans, whose sister has been recently murdered under similar circumstances, the stage is set for a showdown of biblically epic proportions. As they wend their way through lies and deception in search of the truth, the pair will encounter darkness and evil they could have never dared to believe is real.

From underground Dark Web sites showcasing brutality the likes of which has never been seen, to Manhattan boardrooms and basements concealing depravities of the foulest kind, Neville and Fiona find themselves in a battle for their very lives and souls.

Just when it seems like all is known, a twist of fate ramps up the terror even further…securing the dread right to the very last page…

"An unrelieved orgy of sadism." —*Variety* on *Night of the Living Dead*

AVAILABLE NOW

ABOUT THE AUTHOR

With twenty books published internationally and nineteen feature movies in worldwide distribution, John Russo has been called a "living legend." He began by co-authoring the screenplay for NIGHT OF THE LIVING DEAD, which has become recognized as a "horror classic." His three books on the art and craft of movie making have become bibles of independent production, and one of them, SCARE TACTICS, won a national award for Superior Nonfiction. Quentin Tarantino and many other noted filmmakers have stated that Russo's books helped them launch their careers.

John Russo wants people to know he's "just a nice guy who likes to scare people" -- and he's done it with novels and films such as RETURN OF THE LIVING DEAD, MIDNIGHT, THE MAJORETTES, THE AWAKENING and HEARTSTOPPER. He has had a long, rewarding career, and he shows no signs of slowing down. Recently his screenplay for ESCAPE OF THE LIVING DEAD was made into a five-part comic book released by Avatar to great acclaim; it made the Top Ten of Horror Comics nationally and spawned two graphic novels and ten sequels.

Russo's latest horror novel is THE HUNGRY DEAD, published by Kensington Books. And his new mainstream novel, DEALEY PLAZA, has already garnered 13 Five-Star reviews on Amazon. He is also slated to direct two movies: a remake of his cult hit, MIDNIGHT, and a brand new take on the "zombie phenomenon" entitled SPAWN OF THE DEAD.

His popularity among genre fans remains at a high pitch. He appears at many movie conventions each year as a featured guest, and he considers his appearance at the Orion Festival 2013, hosted by Kirk Hammett and METALLICA, one of the highlights of his career.

Made in the USA
Monee, IL
23 April 2022

95277498R00118